D0323419

F
BAS

Bastable, Bernard

To die like a
gentleman

$16.95

DATE			
10 27			
2-21			

FICTION BASTABLE, BERNARD
BASTABLE

TO DIE LIKE A GENTLEMAN

TO DIE
LIKE A
GENTLEMAN

BERNARD BASTABLE

TO DIE
LIKE A
GENTLEMAN

St. Martin's Press
New York

Library of Congress Cataloging-in-Publication Data

Bastable, Bernard.
To die like a gentleman / Bernard Bastable.
p.   cm.
ISBN 0-312-09402-7
1. Great Britain—History—Victoria, 1837-1901—Fiction.
I. Title.
PR6052.A665T6   1993
823'.914—dc20   93-19384   CIP

First published in Great Britain by Macmillan London Limited.

First U.S. Edition: August 1993
10   9   8   7   6   5   4   3   2   1

TO DIE
LIKE A
GENTLEMAN

CHAPTER ONE

The Governess

Miss Frances Weyland to Miss Elizabeth Page

My dearest Lizzie,

My emotions as I left dear, dear Merton Hall I will not attempt to describe. You, my closest friend, will understand – though even you, with a loving mother and a brother and sisters, cannot *quite* enter into my feelings. Enough to say that for the first ten miles kind Mr Jones gave up trying to make conversation, and did his best to look the other way – as far as he could, whilst at the same time driving the cart!

But that is far behind me, and the first thing I must tell you, to relieve your fears, is that I do believe my 'lines are fallen in pleasant places'. I am not referring merely to Elmstead Court itself, of course, though the grounds are splendid – somewhat shady and overgrown at the back of the house, but with a fine rose garden and some glorious walks and fine prospects as soon as you come further away. No – it is not the house to which I am referring: it is in the family itself that I feel I have been most fortunate. It is no doubt true, as your mama said, that Sir Richard's father was in trade and manufacturing all his life, but nevertheless nothing could be clearer than that Sir Richard himself is a thorough gentleman – a thorough English gentleman, of a kind that seems to be fast dying out. This was borne in on me on Sunday at church, when I saw him

surrounded by his family, his household, and his tenants –
indeed by his own vicar: there was something fine and simple
in the thought of his being the centre of so much life, of his
possessing so much beneficent power, and being the cause of
so much happiness and contentment. I confess that the thought
of my being a small part of it did me good.

But indeed I was conscious of being part of an exceptionally
well-bred circle from the first moment I arrived. At my first
dinner, for example (I had only arrived two hours before, but
I had been allowed to warm myself by a *good fire* in my own
room), not only was I treated with conspicuous courtesy and
attention throughout the meal by Sir Richard and Lady
Hudson, but at one point the master of the house singled me
out by raising his glass and inviting me to drink with him. The
fact that I would *very* much rather he had not done it, being
overcome with embarrassment, and unwilling to do more than
sip my wine, does not lessen the kindness of the gesture. And
how unlike it was to my first dinner at Sedgwicks', when I was
ignored by the whole family from start to finish of the meal! I
feel most acutely how fortunate I have been in making the
change.

Sir Richard is a well-looking man: not tall, but well made;
very dark, wavy, strong hair, yet altogether delicate and
fastidious in his ways. Your mama, I remember, said he was a
connoisseur, and this is how he affects the observer. Lady
Hudson looks younger, perhaps not over forty, and still a
handsome woman, in spite of running to stoutness. Though so
decidedly attractive, she is certainly a motherly person, and
most concerned about her children and their progress, being
untiring in her enquiries about their proficiency and her
suggestions about their respective characters, which are always
acute. Of the girls I will say more when I have had greater
opportunities of observing their accomplishments and of
thoroughly knowing them, but at the moment I am determined
to be pleased with them. They have been kind and attentive
towards me, and there seems to exist a perfect confidence
between them and their mother.

The boy is aged, I would hazard, fifteen or sixteen, and has his own tutor, of course. Mr Worsley is a quiet, respectable young man, a graduate of Cambridge, I believe. Now don't be fancying romances, pray, dear Miss Eliza, as you did so *unfortunately* with your poor brother James, who no more thought of me than of the Queen herself, nor I of him more than the Man in the Moon! You have an imagination decidedly too active, and especially so in a certain sphere! So far there have passed few words between Mr Worsley and myself, and nothing at all that might be dignified by the term conversation. On matters scholarly he would think me too inferior in accomplishments to himself to merit consultation, and on other matters we merely 'pass the time of day'. Which is exactly as it should be. What could be more imprudent, nay, impossible, than for a poor tutor and a poor governess to join their poverties together in holy matrimony? The young man is civil, pleasantly civil, and nothing more.

Sir Richard, I suspect, is a strict father to his son, perhaps too strict – but how preferable that is to the *modern* system of indulging the young, as I saw it in practice at the Sedgwicks'! Better, better a thousand times, too much control than too little! And how vividly one fears the consequences in the later lives of the Sedgwick children! Between the boy and his tutor there exists, I fancy, a warm feeling and a strong mutual regard, and I would conjecture that Mr Worsley somewhat mitigates the sternness of Sir Richard and renders the young man's life much more tolerable than it would otherwise be.

All these, pray remember, are but *first impressions*.

To sum up, dear Lizzie, I feel sure that I have come to an *interesting* family, and one that wishes to behave properly as well as generously towards the educators of their children. More, no doubt, will become clear with time, but it is already evident that my stay here (which can hardly be more than four or five years, I think, since the youngest daughter is already thirteen, and Lady Hudson is hardly likely to have more children, though a youthful-looking woman, as I have said) – my stay here, I say, will be of a quite different character to my time of *bondage* among the Sedgwicks. One little indication: because the family treats me with proper consideration, the servants do likewise. None of the ill-bred familiarity of the Sedgwick domestics! The butler is very old and has served Sir Richard since he came to Elmstead Court. I fancy I am already something of a favourite with him, and he has more than once saved me from embarrassment at meal times, due to my unfamiliarity with dishes and customs. Sir Richard seems to treat his household well, and he is much respected. He is especially dependent on an under-footman, who attends him at times when the gout plagues him (and who, no doubt as a consequence of this dependence, is the one servant who may be said not to know fully his place). This gout of Sir Richard's is intermittent but severe. 'Hereditary, alas,' he said to me this morning when I met him in the hall, leaning on Joseph, the said footman: 'not something, sadly, that I can regard as divine retribution for any excesses of my own.'

He smiled wryly at this, and I was obliged to do likewise. He has an odd sense of humour at times, which I do not entirely know how to respond to.

My dearest Lizzie, give my kindest love, and most grateful thanks, to your mother, and to your dear sisters, especially little Ellen, who became a great favourite with me in my too short stay at Merton Hall. If I send any greeting to your brother, you, my suspicious little puss, will misinterpret, and consequently I send none. But how often do I *think* of my time among you all! How I recur to it as I go off to sleep, in spite of the happiness and contentment I feel here! You are all, to me, like my family now – are the only family I shall ever know! Until we meet again – when, when will that be? – I am,

your ever-loving friend,
Frances

CHAPTER TWO

A Gentleman's Home

The long polished table in the dining room at Elmstead Court reflected a heavy and hideous epergne, a candelabrum of many branches and the dancing light from its candles, and the shadowy forms of Pennywear the butler and Joseph the footman and man-of-all-work, whose movements around the table caused the light to leap and flutter, and their reflections to dance. It reflected too the family of Sir Richard Hudson, Baronet.

It reflected three Miss Hudsons, whose ages ranged from thirteen to eighteen, all well formed and becomingly dressed, in a far from provincial style. Miss Jane, the eldest, was decidedly the most intelligent looking, Miss Amelia and Miss Dorothea being merely lively in appearance.

It reflected the heir to the title, Andrew Hudson: adolescent, a little shy, a little subdued, his eyes fixed most often on his plate. It reflected too one tutor and one governess, both deferential and quiet.

It reflected – most of all it reflected – Lady Hudson herself, whose jewels jigged with light and caused a riot of reflections, gorgeous to behold: a woman of handsome shape, with fine brown eyes and a bearing which was confident at most times, though least so when she addressed her husband.

And the table most darkly reflected Sir Richard Hudson himself: substantial, dignified, his face strongly marked and lined – by pain, perhaps. His hair and heavy eyebrows were black and thick, his eyes authoritative and sharp. His voice, when he spoke, suggested that the possibility of his being interrupted before he had had his say out did not occur to him. He spoke precisely, slowly, decisively.

'Mr Peel,' he was saying, 'is proving to be the man for the hour. Mr Peel is surprising us all. As one who has always been a friend to reform and an enemy of outdated institutions I confess myself confounded in my expectations. And I believe Her Majesty is as surprised and pleased as the rest of us.' He smiled around the table, a low-powered smile. 'I believe I break no confidences if I tell you that I was speaking last week to Lord Ogmore – equerry to the Queen Dowager, you know – I was speaking, as I say, to Lord Ogmore on matters of business, and he informed me that Her Majesty was most taken with Mr Peel personally, and had the most complete confidence in his conduct of affairs. It is satisfactory to know this because' – his dark eyes sparkled a little – 'things have not always been so easy in that quarter.'

He eased his shoulders back in his chair, having finished. Joseph came forward to fill his glass.

'Ah, the bed-chamber ladies,' murmured Lady Hudson.

'Precisely, my love.'

'The Queen was surely ill advised to take the stand she did on that matter,' said William Worsley, the boy's tutor.

'Ill advised,' repeated Sir Richard, his mouth twisting slightly. 'There you have it most precisely, Mr Worsley. The rest of us do foolish things, but the monarch is ill advised. Is that not so, Miss Weyland?'

'Oh yes, of course.' Frances Weyland spoke quietly, confused as usual when addressed directly. 'You put it very well.'

Sir Richard looked into her face, which was blushing slightly in confusion. Then she lowered her face to her plate. Sir Richard smiled bleakly at Mr Worsley. Then he eased himself forward in his chair again.

'I think we can say, albeit with hindsight, that Sir Robert's use of his office is precisely what we should have expected of him,' he continued, the half-smile on his face fading slowly. 'His conduct over Catholic Emancipation, though most of us were bewildered by it at the time, now seems an act of the most far-sighted statesmanship. It was like the Act of Union – a piece of work that was the subject of inglorious controversy and disgrace-ful wrangling during its inception, but which, once done, no one in their senses would contemplate undoing. When was the Act of Union between the two parliaments, Andrew?'

The boy looked up abruptly, blinking.

'Seventeen hundred and . . . nine, I think, Papa. In the reign of Queen Anne.'

His voice was very low, as if embarrassed at having to speak out, even before his own family.

'Seventeen hundred and seven. It does no harm to be accurate in such matters. A young man with a Scottish name – your fault, my dear – might well be expected to know the date on which that country lost its independence.'

'I cannot think why you should say his being called Andrew is my fault, Richard,' said Lady Hudson, sounding a little flurried and uncertain of what she was being accused. 'You never told me you disliked the name.'

'Nor do I, my love. But you remember that at the time of Andrew's birth you had a romantic passion for Scotland, brought on, I fancy, by reading the novels of the good Sir Walter. You also had expectations from your Uncle Andrew, I remember, and hoped to please him by naming the boy after him.' He looked around the table, as he always did when he was about to say something good. 'You were cured of the romantic passion by the weather during our one and only holiday in Scotland. And you were cured of the expectations during the reading of your Uncle Andrew's will.'

Polite laughter was ready, and rippled round the table. Sir Richard once more leaned back in his chair.

'You must not take your father seriously,' said Lady Hudson to her children, now satisfied that her husband was in a good mood. 'I hope I am *not* the sort of woman who worries her life out hoping for legacies from her relations.'

'You are not, my dear. I pay you the compliment of saying

7

you are guiltless of that. As, indeed, you are guiltless of receiving any.' Once again there was a ripple of laughter. Sir Richard's tiny smile indicated satisfaction. He turned towards his wife and nodded, which Lady Hudson took as a signal to rise. She led from the dining room her son, her daughters, and Miss Frances Weyland. Joseph, standing by the door, watched the downward looks of all but the lady of the house with something almost like a smile on his face. Then he shut the door, and came back to stand at his position by the sideboard.

'A glass of port, Mr Worsley,' said Sir Richard, passing him the decanter which Pennywear had placed in front of him.

'Thank you, sir.'

His inclusion in the ritual of port was something that clearly pleased Mr Worsley, for it was the time of day when Sir Richard most nearly spoke to him as an equal.

'I flatter myself,' said the master of the house, setting his glass down, 'that Miss Weyland will be writing my little words of wisdom concerning the monarch home to her mama this evening, with appropriate commentary on the soundness of my judgement.'

Mr Worsley smiled, as if he were part of a male conspiracy.

'I fear you must make do with her commonplace book, sir,' he said. 'I believe she has no family.'

'Indeed?' said Sir Richard, raising his great eyebrows. 'But no doubt I should have guessed. Governesses have no families. Which I suppose is why they are such a knowing species of gentry.'

'Would you say that Miss Weyland was knowing, sir?'

'Oh – a seeing, spying, guessing, planning sort of young lady, I've no doubt of it. Very knowing indeed, without' – he paused and raised his glass to the light – 'without knowing it.'

Mr Worsley smiled again, cleverly realizing that a laugh would have been excessive.

'Well, I'm sure you are right, sir,' he said, 'and I shall be on my guard.'

Sir Richard bared his teeth in a not too pleasant smile.

'If Andrew had been a mite older,' he said, 'it's him I would

warn. A knowing governess may yet nourish impossible dreams.'
He laughed, down the bass scale, and emptied his glass. As
Pennywear bent forward to fill it again, Sir Richard sighed,
meditatively. 'I suppose before long we'll have to keep the lad
with us for port,' he said, pushing the decanter once more in Mr
Worsley's direction. He shook his head. 'Dull, decidedly dull.'

'Thank you, sir,' said Worsley, pouring himself a small glass
with Sir Richard's eye on him. 'I think you misjudge the boy, if
I may say so, sir. He is a most gratifying pupil to teach, and I
find him in many respects highly intelligent.'

'I was not referring to the boy, Mr Worsley, but to the conversation we are to have in the boy's presence. We must rein in our
tongues. He has been cloistered, and must learn the ways of the
world gradually. But since you bring the matter up, I think he
is dull. Damnably dull.'

His voice was getting louder, doubtless as a consequence of
the drink, but giving the impression that he wanted to put this
message across to the boy wherever he was in the house.

'He has quite an astonishing grasp of political economy,' Mr
Worsley put in quietly.

'No doubt, Mr Worsley. But my point is that one can be
intelligent and at the same time damnably dull. In fact I have
frequently found that the two things go together, and I have no
doubt I shall find it so with Andrew.' Sir Richard let his voice
become less magisterial. '*That*, no doubt, is the result of giving
him a Scottish name,' he said.

'Cambridge, I am sure, will bring him out,' said Mr Worsley,
with the same quiet persistence.

'You think so? I fear it will only bring out his earnest provin-
ciality. Andrew might shine at one of the provincial colleges. At
Durham he might count as a great brain. At Cambridge he will
seem like a hobbledehoy. For all your excellent endeavours, Mr
Worsley.'

In the drawing room Lady Hudson was pouring tea.

'So good of you, Dr Packenham,' she said. 'I know Richard

will appreciate your visit, though perhaps he will not show it, for he always says that the only thing to be done under these attacks is to wait for them to pass.' She handed him his cup, with a tolerant smile for the whims of her husband. She looked astonishingly young when she smiled.

'So many of my patients expect miracles of me that it is a considerable relief to come across one who expects nothing at all,' said Dr Packenham. He was a tall, positive man, with a firm bedside manner, handsome of feature, a little too smooth.

'Perhaps you would be so kind as to take these to Jane and Miss Weyland,' said Lady Hudson, handing him two cups. 'Joseph is attending on Richard as usual: he becomes quite indispensable to him during these attacks.'

Frances Weyland and the eldest Miss Hudson were seated in the drawing room's window seat, their heads bent over a copy of *The Lady's Keepsake Album*. The younger members of the family were not obliged to come into the drawing room after dinner. Dr Packenham carried the two cups over with a smooth, benign air, as if they were approved medication.

'Butlers and doctors have a great deal in common, do they not?' whispered Jane Hudson to Miss Weyland as he approached. The two bent low over their book to hide their smiles, and then received the cups of tea demurely. Dr Packenham, stooping to set down the cups, raised his eyebrows quizzically at the book which was the object of their study.

'You are wicked,' said Frances Weyland, as he glided away. 'And you were well paid back. Dr Packenham despises the *Album*, that he made quite clear.'

'How would he not?' said Jane, her mood seeming to change. 'He is an educated man. Were I an educated woman, I have no doubt I would do the same.'

Her sharp brown eyes sparkled with discontent, and she drank from her cup impatiently.

'I suppose Dr Packenham thinks we should be reading something improving,' said Frances Weyland, shooting a glance not altogether friendly in her pupil's direction.

'What could be more improving for a young lady destined

to be launched upon the fashionable world than a volume of fashionable nothings?' asked Jane, in the same sharp tone. 'Look at this young man – what a type of the love-sick swain! How altogether admirable! Look at the suspicion of a simper about his mouth – how perfectly charming and genteel! I have no doubt I shall meet twenty or thirty perfect replicas of this young man in London next month.'

Frances Weyland seemed not to be listening.

'There is a look – a slight look – of Mr Worsley about him,' she said.

Jane looked again.

'Then most certainly there can be no simper.'

'True. He is a model tutor, and eminently serious. How long he and Sir Richard are over their port. What do they talk about, I wonder?'

'Men's business. What else but the sort of thing they feel is unsuitable for women's ears? Anything at all which calls for sharpness, penetration, intellect, knowledge of the world. Oh, I have no doubt they find plenty to talk about!'

Frances Weyland let a moment or two of silence elapse after this as if in reproof.

'I imagine your father is starved for male company during these terrible attacks.'

'He has Joseph.'

'I meant, of course, male company to whom he can *talk*,' said Frances. Jane smiled, secretively. 'We must all hope that Sir Richard's attack will soon pass,' continued Frances. 'I hope there is no worsening of the symptoms to be feared from Dr Packenham calling so unexpectedly.'

'If, indeed, it is my father that Dr Packenham has called to see,' said Jane, looking towards the sofa.

'Dear Dr Packenham,' said Lady Hudson, putting her hand briefly on to his. 'You are too attentive, indeed you are. I assure you, I am perfectly well, and looking forward to our little season in London. There is nothing to fear on my account.'

'You will be a great loss to the neighbourhood,' said Dr Packenham, looking at her meaningfully.

'Oh, we shall be away so short a time – a month! – nothing at all. We shall not be missed, I am quite sure. It is only because it is three years since we had any lengthy stay in London that you can think any such thing.'

Dr Packenham sighed.

'No doubt much of your time and energy will be taken up with looking after Sir Richard,' he said, none too sympathetically.

'Oh, Richard will have Joseph, as usual. Besides, I expect he will be perfectly well. They never last more than a month, these attacks. Richard in London will be as he always is – active and energetic, lobbying members, making contact with the new government. I imagine I shall only see him at breakfast.'

'I meditate,' said Dr Packenham, 'a visit to London myself. If I can procure a satisfactory *locum tenens*.'

'How exceptionally pleasant!' said Lady Hudson, smiling at him brilliantly. 'And how good it will be for you to get away from Elmstead for a while. Too much sickness is depressing, even for a doctor. We shall expect to see you constantly in Woburn Square – we shall insist upon it!'

'I shall hope to have that pleasure,' said Dr Packenham softly. At that moment his ear caught the sound of Sir Richard, heavily walking the length of the hall. Dr Packenham lightly got up from the sofa and placed himself negligently by the fireplace opposite Lady Hudson, cup in hand.

Sir Richard came in slowly, cautiously, leaning his whole weight on the stalwart Joseph, who was dextrous in manipulating the doors and guiding him – painful step by painful step – towards his favourite chair.

'Packenham,' said Sir Richard. 'A real pleasure.' He sank gratefully into the depths of his chair. 'Don't tell me – that I should sit – in an upright chair – and that I'll never get out – of this one.' At last he was comfortable. 'I have no doubt you would be right as usual. But while I am down, I prefer to be comfortably down. To get up, I shall rely on Joseph.'

'I've never known a patient on whom good advice is so wasted,' said Dr Packenham, genially. 'I should not like to be your spiritual adviser.' As Sir Richard shot him a quick glance at this, he went on, rather hurriedly: 'And how *is* the patient today?'

'As ever, as ever. Don't waste your professional concern on me – I shall be ill until I am well: there is no more to be said. Concern yourself with Lady Hudson, my dear man. She's been looking out of sorts recently. Or, better, entertain her: it's possibly nothing more than boredom.'

'Out of sorts, Lady Hudson?' said Dr Packenham, turning to her with the correct degree of professional concern on his face.

'Perfect nonsense, Dr Packenham,' said Lady Hudson, pouring her husband a cup of tea and handing it to Joseph. 'I have been looking nothing of the sort. You know very well that Richard always tries to divert attention from himself when he is suffering from these attacks. Really, he should have been a dog, you know – so he could just slink off to be alone when he is in pain.' She glanced briefly at her husband to see how he was suffering these remarks, and seeing no sign of a thundercloud she went on: 'You remember when he pretended to fear all the girls were suffering from consumption, purely to take your mind off his own ailments?'

'It was fortunately very easy to establish the fallacy there,' said Dr Packenham, bowing in the direction of Miss Jane.

'And as to boredom – you know perfectly well, Doctor, I have far too much to do to feel anything of the sort.'

'I can vouch for that, at any rate,' said Packenham. 'Your concern – your practical concern – is very much appreciated among the poor.' He turned to Sir Richard. 'I met Lady Hudson only last week, down among the cottagers, most generously ministering to the needs of old Sally Birley.'

'Pauperizing her, as usual,' said Sir Richard, smiling briefly. He took another sip of tea, and handed his half-empty cup back to Joseph. 'Old Sally Birley – that's the old *blind* woman, is it not?'

*

13

'Please don't put aside your book,' said William Worsley, who had followed Sir Richard inconspicuously into the drawing room at a respectful distance. 'I shall merely drink a cup of tea, and then go to my pupil.'

'We shall most certainly put away our book, Mr Worsley,' said Jane Hudson, so positively that Frances Weyland glanced at her, as if in reproof. 'We have been reading it only because there was nobody to talk to. And please don't too obviously despise the volume in question, because it is a purchase of Mama's, and to do so would be disrespectful.'

'I had no intention of reflecting on your choice of reading,' said William Worsley, smiling tolerantly.

'Though it is, to be sure, abominably silly, is it not, Miss Weyland?'

'It whiles away an hour,' said Frances Weyland, smiling charmingly at her pupil, and showing a very good profile to William Worsley. 'I should be sorry to need it to while away a day.'

'And what would you choose to while away a day?' asked Mr Worsley, but turning to Jane Hudson. She shrugged.

'Mrs Trollope's latest – the eternal Mrs Trollope's latest. Or Mr Ainsworth, if I could remove him from Papa's study without fear of his discovering his loss.'

'Jane!'

'Or Mr Dickens, if the book has not already been ruined by Papa's reading it aloud.'

'Jane!' said Frances Weyland, more urgently.

'You are indeed unkind,' said William Worsley. 'Your father reads aloud quite excellently.'

'Oh yes, excellently,' said Jane calmly. 'All fathers of families are universally allowed to do that. And I fully admit that Papa is better than most. But in the serious style. Sir Walter I can listen to with much pleasure. But not Mr Dickens. Papa is not made for the humorous style.'

'You are most unfair tonight, Jane,' said her governess. 'Sir Richard likes his jokes more than most of us.'

'He most certainly has humorous notions,' admitted Jane, looking in her father's direction. He was being handed a refilled

14

cup, and was taking the opportunity of Joseph being bent over him to whisper something in his ear. 'Who else would choose to spend the whole day in the company of Joseph? Oh yes – I have to admit it: my father *has* his humorous side.'

As they watched, Joseph straightened, inclined his head, and withdrew some distance behind his master's chair. He was very large, and about his heaviness there was a suspicion of brutality, of an animal keeping its ferocity tightly in check. But he stood quite stiff, passive, imperturbable, as the conversation around his master flowed on.

'I have never liked Joseph,' said Jane Hudson quietly.

CHAPTER THREE

The Tutor

FROM *The Beauties of Hampshire* BY A GENTLEMAN OF LEISURE, PUBLISHED BY CHAPMAN AND HALL, 1855

Elmstead Court (formerly Elmstead Manor) is a substantial residence built in 1775, in a classical style that the taste of today will find a trifle cold and forbidding. The name was changed in 1825, when the house was bought by Josiah Hudson from the Nicholson family, whose fortune had been depleted by imprudence and the wars against Napoleon. Mr Hudson (shortly afterwards elevated to a baronetcy) did not find country living to his taste, and almost immediately returned to his native northern counties, leaving his son to perform the duties and exercise the rights of Squire.

I have not seen the interior of Elmstead Court, the house being generally closed as its present owner lives abroad. It is said to be tastefully furnished and decorated in the style of the previous age, and to contain pictures acquired by the late Sir Richard Hudson during his travels as a young man on the Continent. They include a fine Guardi and a reputed Titian. The grounds are extensive. To the front of the house there is a fine drive, forking to form a circular approach in front of the central portico. To the east are a stable block and a somewhat overgrown shrubbery which extends round to the back of the house. Here there are fine lawns, a rose garden, and wilder grounds, handsomely afforested, which extend down to the River Itchin.

The village of Elmstead, picturesque but of no architectural interest, lies three-quarters of a mile to the south.

*

The Tutor

29 April
My pupil's progress towards maturity of judgement continues
to interest me. His grasp of the essential principles of
diplomatic history is astonishing. Our discussion this morning
of the events preceding the Spanish Marriage affair was, it
seemed to me, not inferior in quality to a Cambridge tutorial.
If I flatter myself in this comparison, I am sure I do not flatter
him. Over the last few days, since the incident at dinner when
he failed to remember the date of the Union (for the boy has
a head for *principles*, rather than facts), I have taken the
opportunity to inform him thoroughly on the essential points
of Scottish history. Unluckily Sir Richard has turned his
attention to Ireland.

30 April
I fancy Lady Hudson would be pleased to know that her
daughters had tuition similar in quality to that of her son. Or
perhaps it is the daughters who have taken the matter up with
her, in particular Miss Jane, for Lady Hudson's interest in
Andrew's progress so far has been, not perfunctory by any
means, but of a purely conventional parental sort. Now she
has broached the question of special lessons for Jane in modern
history, with some elementary introduction to political theory.
Of course her suggestions for reimbursement were most
generous. Whether Sir Richard has enough belief in the
education of young ladies to agree to this plan I do not know,
but he is advanced in his political views, and while he may
joke his disagreement, I suspect he will *in fact* concur. Miss Jane,
I am convinced, is chafing against the inadequacy of her
education hitherto – a diet of facts, with none of the larger
vision. *She* would certainly welcome the opportunity of more
stimulating educational fare. The matter would have to be put
with great tact to Miss Weyland. Lady Hudson's suggestion
was in no way meant to reflect adversely on *her* attainments.
She has all the qualifications expected of a governess, and if

her horizons (intellectually speaking) are necessarily limited, they are so by reason of her background and education, not her intelligence. Her predecessor Miss Worth was totally lacking in vision and imagination, and I suspect Miss Weyland finds much to make up, in various directions, in all the girls' training hitherto. She herself, I feel sure, is conscious of her deficiencies in the more advanced areas of her subjects. She feels herself the perfect educator of young ladies, and no doubt for the younger girls *is* so. I believe Miss Jane has a larger mind, a more adventurous capacity, and this could be stimulating to train up, to discipline.

1 May

Sir Richard in great pain tonight at dinner, and everyone very subdued. It is remarkable how he keeps his temper under such affliction. Beyond a savage outburst at Andrew's clumsiness – for the boy *is* clumsy at times, from nervousness, and sudden noise naturally startles Sir Richard and aggravates the pain – he was quiet and forbearing. I startled once, however, a hard twinkle in his eye, which was difficult to fathom.

2 May

I begin to wonder whether the London visit might not be a suitable time to broach the subject of the living of Little Burdock to Sir Richard. How long he intends Andrew to remain under my tutelage he has never said, nor whether he intends to send the boy to university, as, to my mind, he certainly should, for the lad has brains and – incipiently – judgement. (I take his remark about his unfitness for Cambridge to be the product of temporary irritation only.) But in the nature of things the end of my work here cannot be long delayed. The Revd Harmsworth is, I know, far from averse to the idea of retirement, and it is a matter of comment in the village that many things at Little Burdock are being let slide. Sir Richard can hardly be unaware of this, and should be concerned about it. In London he is usually at his best. Mingling with the important and the apparently important ministers to his sense of his own position.

His wife and his eldest daughter are both attractive women, and Andrew, though perhaps shy and socially backward for his years in *manner*, is yet personable enough. Sir Richard believes he himself cuts a figure. He is, in London, habitually good humoured.

Yet how slim are the indications he has given me that he intends the living for me! Hardly more than a mere nod. 'A fine living for the right person.' 'You would do well in charge of a parish.'

Really nothing. Nothing.

Yet I do not believe that the hope that Little Burdock is intended for me is a delusion, or that the expectation is confined to me alone. When, three weeks since, Mr Harmsworth paid Sir Richard a visit on parish business – hobbling most painfully from the dog cart, and presenting something of a parody of Sir Richard's own halting locomotion – he was aided along by the odious Joseph. When the latter came out of the study he met me in the hallway and said: 'Failing, ain't he, the poor old gent? Painful to see, eh?' And he winked with vulgar and familiar significance. Needless to say I stared through him, and gave no indication of having understood his meaning.

Again, when Andrew and I, returning on foot from Upper Heybridge, where we had been inspecting the memorial to a great-uncle of Lady Hudson's (Sir Richard's ancestors, I fear, have no more than Gray's 'uncouth rhymes and shapeless sculpture'), we met up with Miss Weyland and the girls. We fell into converse, and walked in a leisurely manner home. Being perhaps shy of improving conversation, Miss Weyland asked to be instructed on the neighbouring villages and towns. She stood up admirably under Upper Heybridge, Nether Bottoms, Hackem-le-Soken, and Pollock D'Arcy, but when I mentioned Little Burdock she shot a significant glance in my direction.

Even Miss Weyland, then, has heard – little Miss Weyland, who has not been at Elmstead Court above four weeks.

Sir Richard should be willing, when in humour, to give me definite hopes, or else to dash them entirely.

3 May

I begin to wonder whether Sir Richard (and therefore his family) will be able to make the London visit. He looks somewhat improved, but this morning after Dr Packenham had concluded his visit he asked to see Lady Hudson and spent some twenty minutes in the shrubbery with her, talking low and earnest. Doubtless Sir Richard's health is still causing him concern.

4 May

Sir Richard, I fear, is working up to one of his rages with Andrew. This morning at lunch he asked the boy what plans he had for London (for London, I find, is not given up). Now, that the boy *has* plans I know. Not, as might be natural at his age, plans for breaking loose. As I remember myself, not many years his senior, breaking loose in London to memorable effect. For him, as yet, that is scarcely feasible. But he *has* plans, none the less – to see Macready, to attend a lecture series on *Our Indian Possessions*, a subject which interests him greatly, to attend Parliament when in session, and so on. But faced with the direct question, and his father's sardonic eye, the boy could only babble some nonsense about Nelson's Column and Buckingham Palace. Sir Richard said 'Pshaw!' loudly and turned away in disgust.

I wish he would not ask Andrew such things so publicly. If he were to walk with the boy, if that were possible, or talk to him in his study if it were not, and discuss these things casually, without that air of inquisition. But he does not, and these rages of his occur so regularly (though not *frequently*, it must be said) that it might be wondered whether Sir Richard does not rather *invite* them.

If I am right, then the consequences for poor Andrew will be painful, either during or after our London stay. These occasions are painful for me too, in a different way, for can they be otherwise than a sign of dissatisfaction with my work?

And if that is so, what trust would be put in me as incumbent of Little Burdock?

5 May

Miss Weyland has asked my advice on the teaching of foreign languages, French in particular. Very prettily she asked it too. She was especially concerned as to whether the pronunciation of the natives of the countries should be aimed at. I advised against it. This enabled me to broach the matter of the classes for Miss Jane, and she readily agreed in a most sensible manner. As Andrew will be too advanced for any classes Miss Jane could participate in (by reason of her training, not her *intelligence*) it was agreed that Miss Weyland should sit in on the classes, for appearance's sake. She was good enough to say that she expected for herself both profit and pleasure from them. All most satisfactorily arranged, with no tantrums or megrims.

6 May

Sir Richard is much recovered, thank God. He kept to his study for the greater part of the day, but in the evening, as Miss Weyland and I were walking in the shrubbery (our pupils all being on a visit to their old nurse in the village), he and Joseph passed us, he walking almost normally. His expression as he bade us 'Good evening' had a hint of the roguish in it.

London beckons, it seems, in ten days' time.

As he finished the entry for the sixth of May, William Worsley blotted the page, read over the entry, then reached up to his head and pulled out a single hair. This he placed on the page, and then closed the book. He put the book, as usual, under a pile of old schoolbooks of Andrew's, at the bottom of a drawer in his desk in the schoolroom. This was its usual position, and one he suspected that Miss Weyland had discovered. Already that suspicion had led him into rather amusing insincerities in his daily record. For in fact Mr Worsley did not think Miss Weyland sensible, he found her question about the French language (and the pronunciation thereof) distinctly risible, and he did not even think of her as pretty. If he thought she was worth watching, that was on very different grounds.

CHAPTER FOUR

London

MISS FRANCES WEYLAND TO MISS LYDIA PORSON

My dearest Lydia,

It is so long since we corresponded that you will have wondered, I think, at the handwriting on the superscription to this. How well I remember the vows we made on that last memorable schoolday at Whittan Grove, and how ashamed I am at how little we have fulfilled them. Was it you or I, I wonder, who wrote last? If it was you, I must plead that the life of a governess is hard: constant, unremitting vigilance, even when not engaged in teaching or supervising her charges. If it was from the Sedgwicks that I wrote last – I did write to you while I was governess to the Sedgwick *brutes*, did I not? – then you will have some appreciation of what I mean.

When I tell you that the Hudsons – the family with whom I am currently situated – are at present in London, and that I am with them there, you will doubtless be inclined to set me down as an inveterate complainer. But all is not sight-seeing and pleasure-seeking! Sir Richard insists on daily lessons, though he is most reasonable about times, so we fit them in in the afternoons, after mornings spent viewing the sights and spectacles of this *great* and *confusing* Metropolis. I shall say nothing of what we have seen, knowing that you, dear Puss, will by now have seen them long since, nay, even become

ennuyé with the splendour and bustle of our capital. Suffice it
to say that my charges are amazed, excited, charmed by what
they have seen, and I – *I* act the confident, all-knowing
chaperone to the best of my all too limited abilities.

Here in London Sir Richard is the politician, spending much
time in the studies and sitting rooms of the Great, engaged in
matters of importance to himself and others of the landed
interest in Hampshire, whose spokesman he has by his own
abilities become. We see him in the evening, if then – for he
and Lady Hudson entertain much, and on such evenings we
(the children, the tutor, and myself) get our meals as best we
can, very different from the situation when the family is
together at home. Lady Hudson has her own circle in London,
and is naturally much taken up with visiting and seeing the
sights: lectures, concerts, assemblies – occasions to which it
would be impossible and undesirable to take the younger girls,
though Jane, the eldest, sometimes accompanies her mother.
When Lady Hudson is free she occasionally joins our party, as
the other day she did to the gallery in Trafalgar Square. It was
a most happy visit (though *bewildering* from the profusion of
the paintings), and we had the good fortune to encounter a
friend from home (see – a poor governess without family must
call her situation *home!*). This was Dr Packenham, the family's
physician. It was indeed a pleasure to see how unaffectedly he
was welcomed: Lady Hudson is clearly not one to forget old
friends in the whirl and chatter of the great and fashionable
society she moves among here.

Dr Packenham is, I believe, to call tonight. It will be a
sadness not to be able to converse with him, for he has singled
me out for kindnesses before now. My girls will regret it too,
for they have few acquaintances in the Metropolis and, even
amid all the excitement, I see they yearn at times for home.
Miss Jane Hudson, the eldest, professes a distrust of the doctor,
it is true, but this I am sure is no more than a wayward fancy
of youth. She has all sorts of fancies about my poor self and
the equally poor tutor, a sad and hopeless mingling of fortunes
if it were true – which it is not, I assure you.

Dearest Lydia, have you seen Lizzie? I ask because there is not fifteen miles between you and the Pages, and I have had no word from her since I left Merton Hall. I ask because there was a *foolish misunderstanding* which I will not trouble you with recounting shortly before I left dear Merton. Suffice it to say that Mrs Page is a woman too watchful, too suspicious in her ways, ever to be an easy hostess. I should be sad if any false apprehensions she may have conceived should have influenced Lizzie. Pray write and tell me if there has been any foolish talk in the neighbourhood. I would rather know the *worst*, if worst it be, than continue in this uncertainty.

Let us, in short, correspond, as once we promised. Let us vow to be better friends – by letter – in future. Let us outdo Pamela – now *there's* a minx for you! – in the profusion of our confidences. Pray regard this letter as a *new start*.

And remember that I am, dearest Lydia, your loving friend,

Frances

LADY HUDSON TO DR GERVASE PACKENHAM

I do not think we should meet even accidentally too often in society now we are both in London. I want to – God knows I want to. But how can we without raising comment? In the circles Richard and I move in there are spies everywhere – trouble-makers, moralists, enemies of Richard. Whether Richard suspects I do not know. His manner, so withdrawn and ironic, makes it impossible to gauge what he thinks or what he knows. Sometimes I think he would be *pleased* – that he would get a sort of enjoyment out of it. For, believe me, my darling, Richard is a terrible man. Not all the time, not an unrelieved tyrant, but still a terrible man. It is as if – I do not know how to explain – as if he needs from time to time to see suffering, to see someone around him suffering, and to know that he is responsible. Therefore I must be totally discreet.

But I need you. I need to feel you close, to feel your warmth, feel your—— but I must not explain what of you I most want. You understand, my beloved. If we cannot meet too often in society, *in private* we are freer here than in Hampshire. I rely on you to manage it – to arrange *something* so that we may have some blessed times *alone*. Get word to me when you come tonight when and where I may be with you again – one oasis of pleasure in this dismal desert, London.

Do not underestimate Richard – his intelligence, his watchfulness, his will to harm. Beware Joseph.

Ever yours,
(*unsigned*)

EXTRACT FROM THE DIARY OF JANE HUDSON

4 June Academy. Pictures.

5 June Monument. View fine but misty. Weyland talked nonsense.

6 June British Museum. V. boring.

7 June Afternoon concert. Haydn, Beethoven, Hummel, Rossini airs. I might have been a singer, if I had been born into the sphere of life where women *do* things. Weyland sits next to Worsley, *she* contriving things, he v. correct.

8 June National Gallery. Fine pictures. DR PACKENHAM.

9 June Palace of Westminster and Abbey. Debate pompous and dull. Young Mr Disraeli only figure of interest. Abbey crowded. Weyland full of information (from same guidebook I read – Baedeker. She is *not* clever, nor subtle).

10 June St Paul's. Dear God, I am bored with London.

11 June Dr Packenham visits this evening. Dinner guests. Father suggests I should dine, or come to the drawing room after dinner. *Mother opposes*. Does not want me to become *worldly* (!!). I tell them, truthfully, I do not want to dine with them. I remain in my bedroom.

12 June Lessons. To Royal Academy again. Exhibition. London becomes more interesting.

It had not occurred to Frances Weyland on her visit to the Royal Academy with the Hudson girls that it was necessary to watch

Jane closely. Jane had never been any trouble beyond giving her palpitations from time to time at the daring of her views and the force with which she expressed them. Miss Weyland had therefore strolled through the concourse of visitors with her two younger charges, pointing out beauties, real and imagined, in the pictures, and concentrating on things that she thought would interest or amuse them – charming little genre studies, for the most part, of children, puppies, or kittens. Becoming conscious that her eldest charge was no longer with them, she looked back through the mêlée of people and was surprised and shocked to see that she was talking to a young man of about her own age.

He was a far from handsome youth, with an ill-shaped head and spectacles perched on his nose. He was clearly expounding on the beauties of a pleasing seascape – gesturing at it, and showing the finer points of its composition. It looked a harmless enough encounter, but Miss Weyland did not feel it could be allowed to go on for too long. She threaded her way through the throng of people, back towards Jane.

'. . . because it is one of my father's,' she heard the young man say.

'Indeed?'

'But let me show you something else. The Turner is very fine: Napoleon in exile on—'

'Jane!' said Miss Weyland urgently. The two young people turned, caught in a mutual self-absorption.

'Yes?'

'I think you should come with me and your sisters.'

There was a moment's silence, during which the two women gazed straight at each other.

'No,' said Jane. She said it in a voice that brooked no argument from a governess, and she continued gazing at her till Miss Weyland dropped her eyes. Then Jane softened. 'You go on with the girls. We will not be far behind.'

As she walked on with the young man towards the Turner, Jane Hudson was conscious of two things: that he was a young man who was interested in women, who would always have a woman at the centre of his life; and that, interested in him though she was he aroused in her not the faintest spark of romantic feeling. She registered this purely as fact, without any pang of regret or self-questioning. This, she knew, was how she was.

As the young man began his enthusiastic, almost babbling, account of the picture, Jane smiled a little at her victory over Miss Weyland. This, unlike the foolish matter of whether she should dine in company, was the sort of victory she was happy to win. The only victories that mattered were ones that gave greater freedom.

DR PACKENHAM TO LADY HUDSON

Wednesday afternoon at 14 Fulton Drive, off the Edgware Road. Wear everyday dress.

(unsigned)

JOSEPH MORRISSEY TO MRS KATE MORRISSEY

Dear Mother,

At last I got something. I seen something and they cant denie it. Last night after dinner Doctor Packenham put a bit of paper into Her Ladiship's hand as they said goodnight at the door. Sir Richard still in his chair in the drawing room, but I was watching from the door. Frank (footman) never saw a thing. But like you said mother them that watch and see they have all the power. Like you and the duke.

Later Her Ladiship stired the fire, something she never does herself. What price she burnt it. But I saw. Now I know what Im looking for.

your loving son,
Joe

EXTRACT FROM THE DIARY OF WILLIAM WORSLEY

12 June

The London stay, initially pleasurable, begins to be wearisome. Sir Richard enjoys it to the extent that his affliction allows, but I believe the rest of the household will not be displeased to return to Elmstead Court, even the young ladies (who are in any case not of an age to participate fully in London pleasures, and know few people of their own age here).

My lessons with Jane Hudson are productive of great satisfaction, and I believe benefit. She has a strong mind, not unlike her brother's, but more forceful, and I believe that she (like him) chafes against restrictions, in her case the inescapable ones imposed on her by her sex. I know this for a fact because she is surprisingly more open in her resentment of restrictions than he is – he is quiet, thoughtful, careful. Andrew is *waiting*. But then he no doubt sees an end to his condition of subordination, where she cannot. I hope when she grows to womanhood she be not precipitate.

Miss Weyland participates in our lessons, I hope with profit. She always expresses quiet appreciation.

13 June

I sit looking out from my bedroom window in Woburn Square. Andrew has gone with his sisters to Kew. I pleaded a slight indisposition (my interest in botanical curiosities is slight) in order to think out how best I may set about the Little Burdock business.

If Sir Richard is to know of my interest (*hopes* would be too strong a word to use, for he would find it presumptuous), then the subject has sooner or later to be brought into the open. I find I am constitutionally averse to bringing things out into the open, yet in this case I must steel myself. But how? Request an interview in order openly to broach the subject? Hope that an opening will arise in general conversation? The latter clearly would be preferable. Then the subject could be raised almost off-handedly. But what if no such opening arises?

Below me in the street I see Lady Hudson, who has just left
the house – very soberly dressed, no doubt on some charitable
mission. An admirable person in many ways. I wonder if Sir
Richard could be approached *through her*. Now I see Joseph
following after her. Doubtless she has forgotten something. I
fear she is not well organized, not a person of sufficient weight
– or, to be precise, that Sir Richard does not give sufficient
weight to her and her views – for her to be of any use to me.

It will have to be Sir Richard himself, direct.

15 June
Great news! The subject has been opened, and most favourably
received!

And against all odds, I may say. On the evening of the 13th
we all dined *en famille*, the Hudsons' engagements having been
curtailed by reason of Sir Richard's returning discomforts. He
declines to consult London doctors, or to request Dr
Packenham, who is still in London, to see him. All in all he
bears up wonderfully well, but inevitably his temper is at times
short.

At dinner, as so often, Andrew was awkward, flustered, and
failed to do justice to his powers. Talking about our visit to
Hampton Court he was lively, it is true, for on such a subject
his historical sense is roused. But when Sir Richard changed
the subject to Kew (understandably, for he has commercial
interests in both the West and East Indies, and their native
crops have a bearing on the family fortunes), then the boy
stumbled at once, and after a few unlucky misses about plants
indigenous to Jamaica he lapsed into monosyllables. His
father's eye glinted, and he muttered audibly into his wine: 'A
stranger would think the boy half-witted.'

Thus I was not encouraged. But when, over port (Lady
Hudson, Andrew, and the young ladies having left, of course),
he and I continued the train of thought raised by this topic, an
opportunity arose that could not be gainsaid. Sir Richard was
talking of the abolition of the slave trade, of slavery in the West
Indies and Southern states of America, declaring that

legislation was a clumsy instrument, and that what it achieved
might more safely have been left to commercial forces – that
in the longer term abolition would have come about more
satisfactorily as a consequence of the enlightened self-interest
of the slave owners themselves, since it was clear that slavery,
aside from all its other drawbacks and disadvantages, was an
inefficient economic system.

At this point he stopped talking, having said all he wished
to say on this topic. I had agreed with him, naturally, on the
slave trade, but while Joseph helped him to more port I took
him up on one of his phrases.

'Talking of enlightened self-interest,' I said, my heart in my
mouth —

'Ye-es?'

'I have been wondering for some time what you intended,
Sir Richard, concerning the living at Little Burdock.'

There! It was out!

'The living at Little Burdock? Charles Harmsworth's living?'

His voice gave me no encouragement to continue, but I was
now irrevocably launched on the subject.

'It is said he feels himself failing – and is all too aware that
his powers are not what they were. I have been told on all
sides that he feels he must soon retire and go and live with his
married daughter, near Southampton.'

'Really?'

'I have never discussed with you Andrew's future, but it
seems to me that his is the sort of brain that would be enlarged
and sharpened by Oxford or Cambridge —'

'It does?' At this point Sir Richard's far from covert sneer
made me despair of success, and only the impossibility of
drawing back made me go forward.

'It does indeed.'

'If he is to go there rather than to some more modest
institution, it is to be hoped that he will articulate what ideas
he has more cogently for his tutors than he ever does for me.'

'I assure you, sir – against all the evidence of tonight – that
he is capable of that.'

'I am glad to hear it . . .' He softened somewhat. 'I have to
admit that in the past I have sometimes thought of a diplomatic
career for Andrew.'

'Nothing could be more suitable. I believe it is what he wants
for himself. In any case, whatever his future, my work with
him must be over in a year or two's time . . .'

'Ye-es?'

He was not helping me. Perhaps he was playing with me. A
sort of playfulness is characteristic of Sir Richard.

'When that time comes – or even before it – I would hope
to find a more assured, a more stable career for myself within
the Church.'

Sir Richard relented.

'Ah! I have you now, Mr Worsley! You are interested in the
living of Little Burdock for yourself.'

'Yes, sir.'

I said no more. There was nothing more to be said. I hoped
I had said what I *had* said with dignity, but to recommend
myself further to someone in whose house I have been living
for four years would have been a fatuous enterprise. Sir Richard
sipped his port for some minutes in silence. Then he said:

'This needs to be thought on. I've been aware for some time
– and so has the Bishop – that the parish of Little Burdock is
in need of a stronger, younger hand. Leave the matter with me.
It shall not be forgotten.'

I bowed my head and was pleased I had raised the subject.
Naturally I did not expect the matter to be taken up for some
days, perhaps for some weeks. But this very evening, after the
younger members of the family had left the drawing room for
bed, and while Lady Hudson was engaged in discussing
arrangements for a small evening reception tomorrow with
Pennywear the butler, Sir Richard – seated as usual with Joseph
behind him – beckoned me over.

'That business – that Little Burdock business. I've been
thinking it over—'

'I had no intention of rushing you, Sir Richard.'

'Nor I of being rushed, Mr Worsley. Consequently I make

no promises. When we are home, when I have talked to
Harmsworth and the Bishop and to people in the parish, then
it will be time for promises. But it seems to me it might do.'
'Oh, Sir Richard—!'
He held up his hand.
'No promises, and therefore no thanks. If it *did* come to that,
I would expect you to continue responsibility for Andrew. He
was always thought too delicate for public school, and he can
hardly be precipitately consigned to one at his age.'
I did not say that I had never seen any evidence of this
supposed delicacy in Andrew. No doubt his mother worried
unduly after some illness or other.
'Of course,' I said. 'That would be my pleasure as well as
my duty.'
'Either you could ride over, or he could live with you.'
'Yes, indeed. Either arrangement would suit admirably.'
'Ride over, I'd say. You're inclined to be too soft with the
boy . . . And you would need a wife.'
'I beg your pardon?'
'A wife. Half the problems of Little Burdock come from
Harmsworth's having lost his wife two years since. No fault of
his, of course, but there it is. A married man's what's needed
there. Well – don't look so startled, man.'
'The idea is so new, sir . . .'
'Stuff and nonsense! A young man like you not thinking of
the fairer sex? The prospect of Little Burdock should do
wonders for your chances with the ladies. No doubt you have
a wide acquaintance among them . . .'
'Not wide, sir, but—'
'There you are. Think on it. Fix on someone. The parish
needs a woman's influence to back up the incumbent's. There:
given you something to think about, haven't I?'
And indeed he had.

Sir Richard Hudson, aided by the solicitous Joseph, prepared
for bed. In the next room, separated from his by a small dressing

room, his wife and her maid Emily were engaged on the same preparation. He would not be troubling her tonight – not be *pleasuring* her tonight, to put it more precisely, for Sir Richard prided himself that the marital relationship had never been to his wife other than a delightful matter. He had known more abandon, it was true, with women of the night in London in his earlier days, and in more recent ones too, but never more solid satisfaction. But when he was undergoing his spells of illness, the discomfort of his lower limbs compelled him to discontinue that side of marriage for the duration.

And in truth even if he had been well he would not that evening have gone through to her. For he had something to meditate on, turn over and around in his mind, savour.

If someone had said to Sir Richard 'you enjoy power' he would have nodded, accepted it as a matter of course, as something analogous to his liking for syllabub, fine claret, or the smell of ground coffee. His father, who had risen from nothing, had enjoyed power. He had exercised indeed at times something approaching a *droit de seigneur* over the young women who worked in his mills. Other times, other manners. The flavour left in his mind by the memories of his father were crude ones. He was obliged to him, but he did not want to emulate him. His own tastes, like his own life, were more rarefied. Just as he was a country gentleman, with business interests far beyond Yorkshire mills, so his taste was for subtle power, subtly exercised.

Thus it was no part of his plan to seem to promise young Mr Worsley the living of Little Burdock and then at the last moment deny it him. Sir Richard had a reputation for fairness and firmness in the county of Hampshire, and he had no intention of losing it. Nonetheless it was pleasing to think that he had a young man's destiny almost entirely in his control – pleasing to think how he could play with him, decide his fate even in so important a matter as his marriage and his choice of partner. The possibilities in the next few months were endless.

'So our Mr Worsley has finally come out into the open,' he said, as Joseph laid out his nightshirt and began the difficult business of removing his evening clothes.

Joseph chuckled appreciatively.

'No doubt he is lying in bed at this moment,' pursued Sir Richard, allowing Joseph to unbutton his shirt, 'contemplating his blissful future in the married state.'

Joseph's smile was as relishing as his master's.

'I don't know as I've heard that Mr Worsley knows a great many young ladies, Sir Richard,' he said.

'Do you know, I have the same impression,' chuckled his master. 'Not that his tastes lie elsewhere, or I would hardly have kept him on as tutor to Andrew. Merely that he has not hitherto been overly interested in young ladies or the married state. In a stroke I have changed all that.'

'I reckon he must be thinking round on who he knows as he could ask,' said the servant.

'No doubt. Rather like the royal dukes on the death of Princess Charlotte. A little before you awoke to the ways of the world that, Joseph, I suppose. I don't know what George III and his decidedly unattractive queen *did* in the upbringing of their children, but they turned out the most appalling brood of un-desirables this country has ever been saddled with. When poor young Charlotte died, not one of her uncles had a legal brood to ensure the succession, though they had every one of them illicit unions of various degrees of legality, and bastards without number. Europe was faced with the unedifying spectacle of this host of elderly lechers travelling around the Continent in search of princesses ambitious enough, and strong enough of stomach, to accept their hands in marriage. The bait was to provide the heir to the English throne, and even then they were often cheated. The poor Queen Dowager found to her chagrin that she was surrounded by little – or rather all too grown-up – FitzClarences from her husband's previous liaisons, but that she herself was unable to oblige. The Duke of Kent provided us with our present sovereign and promptly died of the effort.' Sir Richard enjoyed pontificating to his servant as to his family, but it sometimes took him rather far from the business in hand. He pulled himself up. 'What were we talking about?'

'Young Mr Worsley, sir.'

'Of course. Currently indulging amorous fancies in the room above us.'

'I wonder you're not afraid of him fixing on Miss Jane, Sir Richard.'

Sir Richard winced as Joseph began the difficult and painful business of removing his trousers.

'I am not in the least apprehensive of that,' he said.

'True, Miss Jane is young to be a parson's wife,' said Joseph, gently inching them down his legs. 'Still—'

'I am not apprehensive because he knows full well that the moment he cast an eye in Miss Jane's direction the offer of Little Burdock would be withdrawn. Mr Worsley is a realist – indeed, he is nothing if not a young man of calculation.' Sir Richard lay back on his bed, relieved of his trousers, and smiled appreciatively. 'You know, Joseph, I fear that the field – to use a vulgar image – will be narrow indeed for him . . . As doubtless he is at this moment realizing.'

Sir Richard's smile had so much enjoyment in it that Joseph determined not to complicate the mood by retailing the information that he had been hugging to himself for some days now. Indeed, the more he thought about it, the more he wondered whether to inform his master at all. There is more than one use to be made of information, he had realized.

CHAPTER FIVE

Proposals

It was generally understood in 10 Woburn Square that the visit to London was drawing to its close. There was no great feeling of sadness about this. The younger girls felt they would enjoy a London of dances and parties when the time came, but they had had enough of the London of museums, galleries, and educational visits. Jane had found enough of interest in the latter days of the stay to dispel the boredom of the early weeks, but now she wanted to settle down again in a familiar setting and meditate what she wanted to do with her life. Andrew suspected that he would one day feel a part of London, at home in it, but that would be when he had an independent existence and independent means. An unpleasant presentiment of what was likely to befall him after they returned to Hampshire underlined the fact that he had not yet reached that state.

But first the Hudsons were to have a treat. They were to go to the opera.

A play would perhaps have been more suitable, more generally enjoyed. But the opera was infinitely more fashionable, and Lady Hudson was determined that the girls should have a glimpse of the world of fashion. Maybe the subtle coolness that had existed between Jane and herself since she had declined to have her down to dinner with Dr Packenham influenced her in this. She knew that Jane was of an age when she could expect to dine with the adults of the family if she cared to, and she had found it difficult to justify her opposition. She could hardly say she did not want another sharp eye watching her. But she was already wondering how much the possessor of that sharp eye had guessed. Lady Hudson was sensitive to atmosphere, and generally liked her relations with other people to be unclouded. Thus she had determined that the 'treat' was to be a particularly splendid and adult one.

Sir Richard was not to go. Even if they had sat in the stalls he would have had to be helped to his seat, and he declined to be made a public spectacle. Mr Worsley cried off, on the grounds that he 'was as near tone-deaf as made no difference'. Sir Richard's eyes glinted at this: he had heard Mr Worsley sing in church, and he knew it was not true. He smiled an inward smile, conjecturing that Mr Worsley had some letters to write.

'You will have to be the man of the party,' he said to his son, in an authoritative way that as usual verged on the threatening. He had seemed throughout the London visit to be making it his mission to rob his son of self-confidence.

But Andrew nodded, as if he did not hear the undertones. He felt he could be the man of the party. In fact, he never lacked for confidence when his father was not present.

The carriage was waiting outside for them at seven thirty. The carriage had come with 10 Woburn Square, which the Hudsons had rented from a family which had made a precipitate retreat to the Continent, where they asserted their breeding in the traditional way by ridiculing everyone and everything on the grounds that they were not British. Their carriage, however, was most commodious, and Andrew, sitting in it, felt intensely and self-consciously alive. He was aware (as young men like him always were) that though he was five foot seven he nevertheless looked younger than he was, but for once he did not mind. Looking out at the streets still bathed in daylight he noticed everything, and he noticed that his sisters' governess, from her inferior position in the depths of the carriage, was doing the same.

Miss Weyland, he thought to himself, is brighter than Mr Worsley realizes. For his tutor's assessment of the governess, though never openly discussed, had been made clear to his pupil by gestures, by the raising of an eyebrow, by remarks that held hidden ironies. Andrew thought that, whatever the deficiencies of her academic attainments, Miss Weyland was quick on practical matters, observant, and rather clever at gauging the main chance and pursuing it.

Within ten minutes they caught their first glimpse of Covent Garden. Its front seemed enormously long and grand, and its bas-reliefs and its massive central columns made it appear to Andrew something nobler than a theatre – a temple, perhaps. Years later, on his first diplomatic posting, he felt something similar about some of the theatres of St Petersburg. Jane was even more affected: when the theatre burnt down in the fifties she wept, as she had never wept for people she had lost. The younger girls simply stared, wide eyed, as if wondering whether this was a theatre or a palace.

But as soon as they drew up in front of the façade it was all bustle. The coachman helped them down, and they moved through the vestibule and up the stairs towards the private boxes, noticing all the time: Amelia and Dorothea noticing the dresses, Jane both noticing the dresses and listening to the conversation, Andrew noticing behaviour – he was teaching himself how to behave in company and in public. Lady Hudson alone was serene, the proud mother merely: she was not expecting any encounter that evening.

'All the world seems to be here tonight,' Andrew said to his mother in a grown-up voice.

She nodded, suppressing any smile that she may have felt inclined to.

'Meyerbeer is becoming all the rage,' she agreed.

They paused for a moment at the top of the stairs. The saloon, with its classical statuary, took away the breaths of the younger members of the party. It was while they were savouring its splendour that Andrew became aware of a young man who was looking at them. When Andrew turned towards him, he looked rapidly away. Andrew felt mortified: they must have revealed themselves as country bumpkins. Perhaps they should not have paused to take in the room and the throng. He shepherded the ladies towards the auditorium, and did not even draw breath in wonder as he surveyed the great candle-lit horseshoe for the first time.

Mr Worsley was writing letters.

Methodical as always, and cool, he had made a list: Miss Catherwood, Miss Easterby, Miss Mumford, and Miss Brontë. He had meditated sending letters to all four of them simultaneously, but consideration of the embarrassment that might ensue had made him drop the idea. They were all from the north of England, from Yorkshire and Derbyshire, the counties in which he had spent his childhood and young manhood, before the crash which had deprived his father of what money he possessed, as well as the will to live. Mr Worsley was aware that young ladies of respectable parentage could maintain a surprisingly efficient network of communication. For that reason he would use his free evening to write to all four, but he would delay dating and sending three of them.

He was writing to Miss Catherwood first of all. Emily her name was, he seemed to remember. But she was an eldest daughter, so 'Miss Catherwood' it could be. Possibly, being the eldest, she would be worth more than the others. Miss Brontë, too, was an eldest, but quite certainly there was no money there.

Miss Catherwood was a sweet, uncomplicated girl, and the approach to her would be easy. Others on his list, and particularly Miss Brontë, would present more problems.

'My dear Miss Catherwood,' he began

> I do not think you can be aware of how strong an
> impression you made on my mind when, all those years
> ago, you visited my sister in our family home.

He paused. Would it be better to say 'can not have been *unaware*'? And would 'heart' be better than 'mind'? He could not remember having given even the most fleeting impression of being in any way smitten, and he thought her just sharp enough to detect any sign of insincerity. He left 'aware' as it was, but on reflection he thought 'all those years' suggested that Miss Catherwood had been left on the shelf. Unable to think of any suitably vague alternative he changed it to a prosaic 'eight'.

The graces of your mind and person are with me as I write, and embolden me to open a subject by letter which I would very much have preferred to open with you face to face.

By good fortune which I trust is not wholly undeserved, I have prospects in the future of preferment in the Church. By God's grace I hope to carry out my duties to His greater glory, and I believe that both *my personal content* and the good of the parish demand that I take a wife. Do not be surprised, therefore, if I approach you, whose image in my mind's eye is yet so strong . . .

She'll be surprised all right, he thought cynically. The question was, would she be pleased, flattered, amenable?

'I can't understand,' whispered Andrew to Jane, 'why the opera is in German.'

They were standing in the intermission in the splendid saloon outside the private boxes. He was trying not to give the impression to any of the elegant (or at any rate substantial) people standing around that he and his family were up from the country, so he spoke very low. 'Surely it's called *Les Huguenots*? I would have thought it would be in French.'

'But the composer is German,' said Jane confidently. 'A German Jew. Of course it would have to be in German.'

'It's in German because the company is a visiting one,' said her mother, turning aside from genteel nothings with Miss Weyland. 'I never think it matters what language they sing in. I can't make out a word. It's the music that counts, isn't it?'

Jane felt snubbed, and wondered why she minded. When you have no other weapons, she decided, you don't like being wrong. Andrew said doubtfully: 'Yes, but I'd like to have a better idea of what's going on. Though of course I know about the St Bartholomew's Day massacre.'

Then he assumed his most languid and experienced air and looked around him. Really these were the sort of people the Hudsons often met at home, only now more splendidly dressed, and bejewelled and bemedalled. Their talk did not seem to his adolescent sensibility to be any more weighty. As his eyes, hooded by his languid air, raked around the room, he realized once more that they were being watched. This time he got a better view of the watcher: a young man – about his own height or an inch or two taller, dark haired, genteel looking, but with a slack mouth and a listless air. He was perhaps twenty-four or twenty-five years of age, and he was watching them from an alcove. Not just looking at them, but watching them. Suddenly the young man seemed to take a decision, and began walking over to them. Andrew's heart gave a leap: he was unused to unexpected social encounters, and unsure whether he could handle one.

'Lady Hudson?' Close to, Andrew decided, the young man looked handsome, but conceited and weak-willed. 'I hope you will forgive the intrusion. I wished so much to have the pleasure of the acquaintance of you and your family. And' – he bowed in the direction of the governess – 'I already have made the acquaintance of Miss Frances Weyland.'

'Lady Hudson – Mr James Page,' said Miss Weyland, an attractive blush mantling her face.

'My dear Miss Brontë,' began Mr Worsley. It was his fourth letter, and the one written with most hesitations.

I do not know if you will remember our meetings at the home of our friends the Taylors. Those meetings are engraved on my mind from the pleasure I took in the

society of those excellent people, and from the interest that
you aroused in me. I believed – and believe – you to be a
woman of sound principles and a strong sense of duty.

He paused. How far should he go in that line? Somehow it
made the young lady sound far from attractive. He took up his
pen again, and gave her the summary of his prospects that had
been standard in all the letters he had written thus far. Then he
wrote:

I believe it would be wrong of me to speak of *love*, for I
saw in that sharp eye of yours something that would scorn
such affectation. But I believe that a fine and useful
marriage may be based on respect, trust, and affection,
and those three things, believe me my dear Miss Brontë,
you have. I do not ask for a decision now, merely some
indication that you do not reject the idea out of hand. I
await with eagerness your reply . . .

Or would await, should the answers of Miss Catherwood, Miss
Easterby, and Miss Mumford prove negative. He looked back
over the letter with more than usual doubt: there had indeed
been *some*thing in that eye . . .

As he wrote the envelope he realized with chagrin that he was
not even sure he had spelt the young lady's name correctly.

'A friend of Miss Weyland's!' said Lady Hudson, with that
unaffected condescension that was so universally admired. Some
other employers of governesses would have said the same thing
in quite another tone of voice. 'I'm delighted to make your
acquaintance.'

'Brother, in fact, to Miss Weyland's friend,' put in Mr James
Page.

'It was to my friend Elizabeth Page's home that I paid a
brief visit before coming to Elmstead Court,' murmured Miss
Weyland. 'After I left my position with Mr and Mrs Sedgwick.'

'Ah yes, I believe I remember now. That was in—?'

'Norfolk,' said James Page. 'Merton Hall, near King's Lynn. A modest enough house, but with fine grounds. Our family has always had extensive farming interests in the area. Miss Weyland and my sister were at school together, and she was a most welcome guest at Merton.'

'How is dear Mrs Page?' asked Frances Weyland softly.

'Tolerable, though not entirely well.' James Page turned to Lady Hudson, though he seemed still aware of Miss Weyland's scrutiny. 'My mother has a nervous affliction for which the doctors fail to find a name, let alone a remedy. She is low of spirits, and gets sick fancies. But she gets on tolerably.'

'She has my sympathy. So often such sickness is put down by men as mere women's vapourings.'

'Perhaps. But my father, when he was alive, was always most sympathetic — perhaps too much so.'

'Your father is dead?'

'Alas yes, these three years. I feel his loss very much.'

He said this in a smooth, glib way that belied the sorrowful expression his face had assumed. Andrew, from the similarities of their position, was quite certain he did not feel his loss very greatly. He ought to have felt some sympathy for the young man, but he disliked his manner, and disliked the way he talked to Lady Hudson but simpered in the direction of her daughter as he did so. Andrew also felt that Mr Page was aware, quite painfully aware, of Miss Weyland's presence, even when as now he was ignoring her.

'And what are you doing in London, Mr Page?' asked Lady Hudson, with if possible a further access of amiability.

'Much the same as you, no doubt — or rather as Sir Richard. Since my father's death I have looked after my own interests, and those of my tenants. I see the gentlemen at Westminster, and the gentlemen of Whitehall — and even the gentlemen (if that is the word) of the newspapers and journals. No doubt Sir Richard does much the same.'

'Indeed yes. Richard is tireless, in spite of his affliction.'

'Sir Richard is not well?'

43

'A gouty spasm – a regular visitor. It prevents him accompanying us tonight, but he tries to pursue his daytime business, since he is so infrequently in London.'

'I should very much like to call on Sir Richard to pay my respects. Are you in London long?'

'A matter of days – at most a week.'

'Sad to leave at the height of the season.'

'My husband's indisposition, you understand. Our stay was always contingent on its getting no worse.'

'Sir Richard must have great trust in his local doctor, if he prefers the discomforts of travel to putting himself in the hands of a London practitioner.'

'He does indeed,' said Lady Hudson, looking him straight in the eye to avoid looking at her eldest daughter. 'Dr Packenham takes excellent care of him, and has an interest in his welfare that no London man could be expected to have. But at heart I suspect that Richard regards all doctors as quacks.'

'Is Sir Richard too ill to receive a visit from a fellow land owner – albeit one from another county?'

'No – at least not at the moment. The progress of the malady is unpredictable. If it gets no worse I am sure he will be delighted to receive a visit before we leave.'

As the audience began trooping back into the auditorium, Miss Weyland smiled at the brother of her old friend, to show that she too would be delighted to receive a visit. The look caught him off-guard, and he mumbled his farewells less gracefully than he had intended.

CHAPTER SIX

A Morning Call

MISS JANE HUDSON TO AN UNIDENTIFIED
CORRESPONDENT

Dear W.,

You ask for all the details I can give you of the 'curious
situation' in the Hudson household. If I could give you the
details I would no longer find the situation curious. The fact
is, I *know nothing*. I feel something is afoot, but of its nature I
am unsure. I *feel* that the situation, the fortunes of the Hudson
family, is about to change, and to change dramatically – yet
of what value is such a feeling? For I *know* nothing – judge only
by signs, looks, departures from the expected. What I must do
is set down the *facts*, and be in no great rush to draw deductions
from them. These then are the facts, since we spoke at the
Royal Academy and at the National Gallery (that second
meeting, by the by, has made Miss Weyland *exceedingly*
suspicious, and she has plied me with questions as to who you
are, and whether we met by appointment. However, she has
said nothing on the subject to Mama).

Tomorrow is our last day in London, a matter of little regret
to most of us, I suspect, though Miss Weyland – Miss Slyboots
that she is – has enjoyed her greater freedom here and the
greater variety of her life, and I suppose I cannot blame her.

This morning there was much bustle and disorder, as the

greater part of our baggage was sent to Elmstead Court in
advance of us. Servants and porters swarmed around the
entrance hall and stairs bearing trunks and valises, jewel boxes
and packing cases. Father, with Joseph in attendance, sat in
his wheelchair in a central position directing operations.

It occurs to me that the head of the household does not
generally feel the need to supervise removals in this way. The
business could very easily – better – have been left to Pennywear
or to Joseph. But no, there was my father, shouting orders,
directing comings and goings with his stick, for all the world
as if the porters were an orchestra and he was Mr Henry
Bishop. Sometimes I get the oddest of fancies: that my father
is there for Joseph more than Joseph for my father. Or at least
that they have become inextricably connected. If I take my dog
for a walk on a leash, *he* is on the leash, but *I* am on it too.
Do you think one should aim to do without servants? But I
digress.

It was in fact inevitable than an accident should happen. I
was in the door to the library, talking over arrangements for
the afternoon's excursion to St Martin-in-the-Fields with Miss
Weyland, and I saw it happen. Andrew was conversing with
Mr Worsley, who was turned in the direction of the door on to
the Square. They were discussing I know not what, but Andrew
was animated in a way he seldom is when our father is present,
which makes me sure that he had forgotten that he was there.
Two of the servants carrying a trunk came down the stairs, and
to facilitate their passage to the door Andrew backed away,
still talking. He fell over father's bad leg, and father let out a
great howl of pain that must have been heard the length and
breadth of London.

I need not go into the ensuing scene – the names my father
called Andrew, the bitter reproaches for his clumsiness, the
threat that he would soon regret his thoughtlessness. These
were to be expected. I mention instead only one thing that
may be relevant to the 'curious situation' of the Hudson family.
As I say, I saw the accident. I saw Andrew backing towards
my father's chair, I saw the gout-stricken leg that was clearly

in his path, stretched out as it was before my father. I was too
far away, and there was too much noise and bustle intervening,
for me to do anything about it. But my father too, I swear it,
saw the boy backing towards his leg. His name, uttered in a
loud voice, would have been sufficient to arrest his progress.
His stick, too, could have arrested it. Yet the name was not
uttered, the stick was not raised. My father saw Andrew
approaching, saw what would happen, yet did nothing.

Why?

As I say, the air in the entrance hall was for some time thick
with oaths, reproaches, name-callings, and exculpations, but
the atmosphere was lightened by the arrival of Mr James Page.
Or if not lightened, then changed. Mr Page is the young
gentleman known to Miss Weyland whom we met at the opera
the other night. On his arrival my father had his chair removed
to a quiet corner of the hall, and became acquainted with Mr
Page there rather than in the study. In the hall we would all
be around, and my father likes to study people and their
reactions to each other. I rather suspect that he found Mr Page
a ripe object for study.

Mr Page says all the conventional things, and says them in
a conventional way. If I were to set them down they might
sound straightforward, manly, honest. But there is in his
manner a conventional simper, with eyes that wander, seeking
approval from anyone within earshot that makes me sure he
does not mean them. How can I be so certain? Because women
are forced all their lives to say conventional things. Some mean
them, most recognize that this is a condition of their remaining
in respectable society. I recognize his hypocrisy because it
mirrors my own. But mine is involuntary; his is not.

My father kept up a flow of polite chit-chat, while all the
time observing this well-dressed, smooth-talking young
fashion-plate, and the reactions of all of us to him.

'Ah, so you are acquainted with – ah, with Miss *Wey*land?
Really? A friend of your sister – of course. And on the strength
of this you felt constrained to introduce yourself – delighted you
did, young man. Excuse my grimace – my leg – most painful

today. So you have met my children? My daughter Jane – a
young woman now – a terribly *old* feeling it gives me to have
a young woman for my daughter. And Andrew? My *son*? You've
met my *son*?'

This last was said with apparent geniality, but with a hidden
meaning audible to the family. As the conversation – or chit-
chat, as I prefer to call it, of the kind my father deems suitable
for the young – continued on its way I began to notice a
particular direction it was taking.

'Ah – the National Gallery. A superb collection – a national
treasury indeed. You are interested in painting? Jane, my eldest
daughter, is most interested in art – sees things in pictures I
am hard put myself to see . . .' And later: 'You have seen Mr
Dickens then? Spoken to him – indeed! I am envious. A
wonderful talent! Another national treasury, one might say.
We all enjoy the books greatly. I read them aloud as they come
out, though my daughter Jane does not admire my reading.
But then, who could do justice to that wonderful vivacity?'

How did he know my opinion of his readings of Dickens? Mr
Worsley? Possibly. Miss Weyland? I hardly think so, though
that is a still water whose depths I have not yet fathomed.
Perhaps he merely observed my expression during the readings.
But the important point (to me!) is that my name was brought
into the conversation at every conceivable opportunity. And
you of all people will realize that my interest in and
understanding of art was greatly overstated – it was just an
excuse for mentioning my name.

After ten minutes or so Mr Page observed that his visit was
hardly well timed, and made to say his farewells.

'I aim to visit my great friend Fred Paisley, sir, in a week or
two's time – your near neighbour. Perhaps you will allow me
to come and pay my respects to you at Elmstead Court?'

'Ah – Fred Paisley. A worthy young man, I believe, though
I do not know him well. Not a great brain, people tell me. Is
that true? Ah – not a great brain, that's your estimate too. But
thoroughly amiable and worthy. Quite. We shall be delighted
to see you, Mr Page. My family will be delighted to see you.

My daughter Jane frequently complains of the dullness of the neighbourhood. Goodbye for the moment, then. Andrew – see Mr Page to the door.'

So Mr Page was forced to depart without exchanging more than the barest of courtesies with Miss Weyland, who I am sure would have wished to converse privately with him. I can only presume that the hope of having such a conversation was the primary object of Mr Page's visit. Instead of which he was forced to listen to burblings about 'my daughter Jane' in whom he has not the slightest interest, though he smirked often enough in my direction.

Again I raise the question: why? If we put the matter at its mildest, its least reprehensible, my father enjoys playing with people, frustrating their hopes. Hardly amiable, in the case of a poor governess (however much of a minx one may suspect her of being) but not very serious. More unpleasant is the thought that he enjoys inflicting pain. This I have suspected for some time in his relationship with poor Andrew. The scene today has crystallized their relationship for me: he enjoys bringing out the worst in him, leading him into difficulty or disaster. He is also – or so I suspect – playing with my mother, in a way I would not care to go into here.

But the crucial question for me is: how far would he go? He is, to put the matter bluntly, a tormentor. His putting my name so constantly before Mr Page – probably merely to frustrate him – does bring up the question of marriage for me. Would he force me into an abhorrent marriage merely to demonstrate his power over me and enjoy my distress? It is through marriage that men with a taste for tormenting (fathers, husbands) can legally satisfy that taste. My father has some reputation for liberality and enlightened views (that sort of reputation is easily gained). Would he endanger it by trying to force me into a marriage that was hateful to me? I fear that he might well.

And if he did, what would my reaction be? Would I fight or flee?

When we talked so interestingly on our two meetings you

said that what interested you was 'curious cases'. I am now unable to decide whether the Hudson family qualifies as such. Are we exceptional, or really quite normal? At any rate I have , a feeling, as I have said, that the coming weeks will in some way or other be decisive.

I will write no more at the moment except to say that your comments on all this would be most welcome. Write to Elmstead Court, Elmstead, Hampshire. My correspondence is not supervised.

Sincerely yours,
Jane Hudson

MISS FRANCES WEYLAND TO MISS LYDIA PORSON

My dearest Lydia,

Your letter was *most* welcome, if also, as you will understand, *most* distressing. I feel that Mrs Page has acted *wickedly* – I think no word could be too strong – in not only spreading such lies about the county, but in persuading her daughter, my dear friend, to believe them. A young woman without fortune has *only* her reputation as a warrant of respectability, and Mrs Page has done her best to rob me of mine.

I shall write again and write properly, dear Lydia, as soon as we get to Elmstead, but I take up my pen now merely to say that *should* you hear talk of my having resumed acquaintanceship with Mr James Page in London, that you have my permission vehemently to deny this. Our paths crossed at the opera, and we exchanged perhaps five words. He came to pay his respects to the Hudson family, and we exchanged *no* words at all. That is all, and if Mrs Page should see fit to spread further mischievous lies, you have my permission to brand them for what they are.

I love you for your friendship to me, dearest Lydia, and am

your loving friend,
Frances Weyland

A *Morning Call*

MR JAMES PAGE TO MR FREDERICK PAISLEY

Dear Fred,

I know we were never special friends at school, but I hope
you knew that I always had a very special respect for you.
What times those were! Being at Winchester was a privilege
none of us will ever forget. What a day when old Batty received
the products of the sweep's boy's labours on his head! That
was you, wasn't it? Or was it Manners minor? But what days!

Do you know, I've always had a fancy to try the fishing in
Berkshire. Any chance of paying you a visit? I have a special
desire to see you because, as I say, I always felt a great respect
for you, as straight a man as any at school. Write and tell me:
is the fishing as good as they say?

Your old school friend
James Page

LADY HUDSON TO DR GERVASE PACKENHAM

I love you, I love you, I love you. We leave tomorrow early.
Being back at Elmstead Court will make things easier in some
respects, but in others how much *less* easy. In particular my
darling how I shall miss the *freedom* of Fulton Drive, and our
wonderful times together *alone*. If only Richard were *sicker*.
Something – I pray it! – something *must* turn up. One day we
will be happy.

A

William Worsley was writing to the last of his potential brides.

My dear Miss Brontë,

Your kind but firm rejection of my proposal does credit
both to your heart and to your principles. I am
emboldened by its very kindness, which is clearly an
expression of an exceptionally beautiful disposition to raise
the question of whether you would see me and listen to me

were I to make the journey to your charming little
Yorkshire village? I believe that were we to meet, even just
once more, you would

You would – what? Did he think his charms would prove irresist-
ible? He had a high opinion of his talents, but he knew his person
was nothing out of the ordinary. After a second or two's thought
he scored the letter through and crumpled it up. The girl should
have recognized that his was as good an offer as she was ever
likely to get. All that foolish talk about 'love'. What did she know
about it?

CHAPTER SEVEN

A Painful Episode

Mr William Worsley was writing in his diary.

> Not only Andrew but the young ladies too are much improved by their visit to London – their horizons much expanded, their information and experience greatly augmented, together with a touch of sophistication which in their station in life does not go amiss. Much of their improvement in fact can be put down to the excellent work done by Miss Weyland, who is not only a first-rate teacher, but a sweet and gentle girl to boot. She little knows how much faster my heart beats when she comes into the classroom. She little knows when she sits in on my lessons with Jane how I long to seize her and make declarations of a quite unhistorical nature.

Mr Worsley read through the passage. That was quite enough for the moment. As well not to bait the hook too lavishly for a first cast. His written words would supplement the looks of an experimentally tender kind which he had been directing at her since receiving the last of his epistolary rejections. He felt into his head, pulled out a hair, and having placed it in the opened book put the diary itself in its usual place at the bottom of the drawer in his desk.

*

It became apparent soon after the family returned to Elmstead Court that Sir Richard's renewed attack of gout was an unusually severe one, and since it came so hard on the heels of the previous one this gave rise to a general anxiety – though in the case of some at Elmstead the word 'interest' might describe the emotion more accurately. When Dr Packenham was overheard to use the word 'heart' in discussions outside the sickroom with Lady Hudson the word went around, first below stairs and later in the house itself (for Lady Hudson kept her worries to herself, and her family had to hear about it from the servants), that the health of Elmstead's master was deteriorating. The matter was not discussed by the family or their teachers, merely referred to obliquely, or by looks and gestures. Sir Richard kept to his room for days at a time, seen only by Joseph, the maid who did his room, and Lady Hudson. When he did appear, however, he was – though weak and needing assistance – his old self: sardonic, watchful, mischievous. The third of July was one of his good days, and he actually came down to breakfast.

'I feel much better,' he said, leaning heavily on Joseph. 'I've stopped taking that foul-tasting liquid that Packenham has been dosing me with and I've perked up enormously.'

'But Richard, is that wise, when the doctor—' began Lady Hudson nervously.

'Of course it's wise if it makes me feel fitter,' said her husband. 'Packenham doesn't know everything.'

His words were prophetic in the short term, for he came downstairs for three days in a row after that. However – as with so many people who think they know better than their doctors – it was medicine which had the last laugh.

This brief Indian summer of good health for his father inevitably made Andrew Hudson more nervous than ever. While his father had kept to his bed he had blossomed – there had been an access of boyish enthusiasm and confidence, as well as a joyous immersion in his studies. Was there also, perhaps, at the back of his mind a suspicion that he might be master of Elmstead before too long – even if the administration of the estate would have for a time to be in the hands of others? The figure of James

Page, who, he was not slow to ascertain, had been master in his own house at twenty-one, had been before him during his London visit. If this feeling of anticipation was not yet so strong as a hope, it surely was there as a possibility.

At dinner on the second day of his father's restored period of renewed health Andrew felt, as so often before, his father's eyes boring in on him as the family sat down to dinner. He took up his soup spoon and held it in an odd, claw-like fashion.

'Andrew – your hands!' rapped out his father's voice. 'Show me your hands.'

Silently, in the manner of an infant-school child, Andrew unclasped his hands.

'Oh, for God's sake – ink! Can you not even keep yourself clean, boy? Go and make yourself fit for table this minute!'

When Andrew returned from washing and scouring his hands, his face was red, either from shame or from anger. His soup was near cold, but his father had held up dinner so he be forced to eat it. He did so in silence – a silence which enveloped the rest of the dinner table.

'Ah!' said Sir Richard, breaking the silence with forced bonhomie. 'Lamb! English lamb – or perhaps Scottish. And roast potatoes. When was the potato introduced to England, Andrew?'

'In the Elizabethan age. By the merchant explorers.'

There was something of sullenness in Andrew's manner, as if he by now knew his fate, and knew that no exertions of his would avert it. Sir Richard smiled – that smile that his family was finding more and more chilling.

'Yes indeed. Other people had pirates, but we had merchant explorers. I think that if we looked at the conduct of Drake and Ralegh and their like we should see some infamous dealings – eh, Mr Worsley?'

'Undoubtedly, Sir Richard,' said William Worsley, who had in fact taught his pupil an orthodox view of the Elizabethan age and its heroic sailors.

'And the queen herself – a headstrong, quixotic, tyrannical body, who has somehow managed to bemuse historians – a sorry crew! – into awarding her greatness. À propos – I hear news from London that the Queen is once more in the family way. Pray God that this time it may be a prince, and Britain may before too long be ruled by a king, as is natural.'

He looked around the table, hoping for an outburst from Jane, at whom this was particularly aimed. Jane, however, was not to be drawn. She smiled at him sweetly, and denied him the chance to put her down publicly.

'And who, Andrew,' said his father, balked, and returning to one of his favourite topics, 'would have succeeded to the throne if our present queen had died childless?'

'Oh – one of her uncles,' muttered Andrew gracelessly. 'The Duke of . . . Sussex, I think.'

'Great Heavens!' exclaimed Sir Richard, who rightly sensed the boy's sullenness was a challenge. 'The nation was threatened for years with the prospect of having as its king the Duke of Cumberland, and my son is ignorant of his very name. Yet the man was a murderer and a libertine of the worst kind.'

'I think the details of his career were kept from me,' said Andrew, now looking directly at his father. 'I imagined he was a murderer and a libertine of the better kind.'

Andrew's impertinence left his father for once speechless.

'Perhaps we should be grateful that we have a queen,' said Jane quickly. 'Since she saves us from having a man such as him on the throne.'

Sir Richard's eyes narrowed, but he said nothing to her, storing it up. He turned back to his son.

'Unable to name the man,' he repeated, 'who until last year – last year! – was the heir to the throne.'

Andrew could have remained silent, but for once he did not.

'I had gathered from you, sir, that there was nothing good to be said of the queen's uncles. That being so, I preferred to say nothing at all.'

'Are you criticizing me?' asked his father, his voice icy. Andrew shrugged.

'Since I hope to serve the Queen in the future, I prefer not to criticize her relatives now. I am not one of those skin-deep radicals who expect respect from those beneath them, but refuse to give it to those above them.'

The two looked each other straight in the eyes.

'I am not used to being criticized by one of my children at my own table,' said Sir Richard through his teeth. 'It is not something I intend to get used to. My study at six o'clock.'

'Certainly, sir,' said Andrew.

'That was unwise,' said William Worsley to Andrew, when they were back in the schoolroom.

'I have tried being wise all my life,' said Andrew. 'All it has brought me is periodical beatings. What worse effect can honesty have?'

'It can have the effect of getting you beaten much more often,' Mr Worsley pointed out. 'After today's performance you can hardly say your father has no cause.'

'My father beats me when he feels like it. If he beats me more often it will be because he feels like doing it more often.'

'You are fatalistic, at any rate.'

Andrew shrugged.

'What else is there to be?' He looked at the schoolroom clock. 'Do you mind if I just read? I couldn't set my mind to any other work.'

At three minutes to six Andrew shut up his book and rose from his chair. Without looking at Mr Worsley he left the schoolroom and began the walk to his father's study. The walk had never seemed so long, nor the house so silent. Everyone in it seemed to be holding their breath and waiting. Perhaps they were. Everyone in it was aware that the offence this time had been no ordinary one. Along the landing he went, then down the wide oak staircase, hoping his footsteps sounded firm and fearless. Only he, surely, could be aware of the thumping of his heart. He walked through the hall, along the passage, and came to the door to his father's study. It must now be six o'clock. Andrew raised his hand and knocked.

'Come in.'

Andrew opened the door. He saw the chair, familiarly in place. He saw his father, seated forbiddingly in his capacious armchair. And he saw, beside the desk, the figure of Joseph, his shirt-sleeves rolled up to his armpits, flexing a long cane in his large capable hands.

To take his mind off what was transpiring in Sir Richard's study – which he regretted, though he had to concede even to himself that it was richly deserved – William Worsley went to the desk in the schoolroom and once again took from the drawer, from beneath the pile of books, rubbers, pens, and notebooks that covered it, the volume that contained his diary.

To his satisfaction the hair had disappeared.

Later that evening, as dusk gathered, Andrew Hudson walked stiffly, painfully in the shrubbery. Every step he took brought back the events of six o'clock.

He flushed anew, with anger rather than humiliation, at the thought of being beaten at his age by a servant. He blamed himself for his stupidity: he should have foreseen that weakened by illness his father would resort to that. He had never shown any consideration for his son's feelings, so it was not to be expected that he would do so in this instance. Andrew could even imagine that it was Joseph who had suggested it: the smile on his face during his father's preparatory lecture, the relish as he flexed, lovingly, the cane in his hands, his tongue flicking out now and again to lick his full lips – all these things suggested unashamed anticipation. And the pleasure he naturally took had been augmented by the expression of surprise and contempt that had crossed Andrew's face at the sight of him there.

Joseph and his father were close because they shared similar tastes.

He remembered with shame his sobs, his shouts, as the beating had progressed. He wished he could have stood it out, bloodied but Spartan in his silence.

Yet he had not sought mercy. That thought cheered him now. He had not been reduced to begging for mercy.

And he now knew one thing, had crystallized one feeling in his heart: he now could name the emotion he felt for his father. For the first time in his life he recognized hatred.

CHAPTER EIGHT

A Visitor

JANE HUDSON TO AN UNIDENTIFIED CORRESPONDENT

Dear W.,

I am tempted to say that events move apace here – yet on the surface they are much as they have always been. My sisters and I have our lessons. My mother as usual supervises the household and makes charitable visits to the village. On occasion she takes me with her – on visits, I suspect, when there is no possibility of her encountering Dr Packenham. My father, after a period of renewed vigour, is now sick again. Andrew has been beaten. Mr Worsley is paying some attention to Miss Weyland.

Nothing is very new, you will say, in this account, except the last item. How then to account for my feeling that things are moving apace?

Let me start with the things I know best: the view, let us say, from the schoolroom. I did not see Andrew after his beating, but we talked alone next day, in the grounds and well away from the house. It is terrible to feel that one can only talk when one is sure one is not being spied on! Thus, I suspect, must people feel in Russia or Turkey. From whom does this feeling emanate? From Joseph, primarily, and perhaps from some of the other servants, mostly housemaids, over whom he seems to exercise some kind of power. But of course Joseph leads back to my father: Joseph's observations are taken back to him. Sometimes I am reminded of that French King – Louis XI, was it? – in *Quentin Durward*: the spider at the centre of a cruel web.

Even alone as we were, in the open and well away from Elmstead Court, Andrew would tell me nothing about the beating: we embraced, he cried a little, said only that he longed to get to Cambridge, away from this house, away from *that man*. I have no evidence, but I believe the beating was administered by Joseph. But – unpleasant as this is, for Andrew, as representing a new and painful departure – the important thing is what led up to the beating. He showed his scorn for my father publicly, stood up to him at table. In particular he expressed contempt for his supposedly radical political views and the contrast with his tyrannical practice. It was something my father could not ignore. It was, in essence, a declaration of hostilities.

I should perhaps add that the estate is entailed on Andrew.

So what I foresee for the future, if – or rather when – my father should regain his strength, is further attempts by my father to assert his own absolute power within the family, and further attempts by Andrew to resist it. In such a struggle I could not be neutral. But what could I do to help my brother, except express support for his fight – which inevitably will, in the short term, have unpleasant consequences for him? What, oh what, can women *do*?

One thing women can do is be courted. This Miss Weyland is finding out at the moment – no, it is something she has long been aware of! In our history lessons Mr Worsley addresses compliments to her, asks her opinion on historical matters, and gravely discusses her replies, however silly (that word is wrong: Miss Weyland is never silly, but she is, I suspect, ill-informed, so her opinions are vulgar, conventional ones which have no weight). What is more he seeks her out at moments when she is alone, which are rare, since she has Amelia and Dorothea constantly to supervise, but they can be calculated upon – and Mr Worsley calculates! When I see him in the hall or on the landing at certain times of the day I know exactly where he is going, though I do not know what he is going to say.

And Miss Weyland herself? She is a sphinx, a veritable sphinx. Yet I begin to suspect that she is in a quandary. She can hardly *expect* a better prospect than Mr Worsley, yet may she not *hope*? Of this more anon.

Thus the facts of the situation: at her coming here Mr Worsley displayed no interest whatsoever: now he displays a great deal, though covertly. What are the reasons for the change? I have seen of late in the schoolroom, or brought to him by the servants, letters in female hands. O glorious penny-post, that has so many of us writing letters! They are replies to letters of his. Why this sudden interest in the female sex? Mr Worsley's hopes for a living from Sir Richard, and in particular the living of Little Burdock, are by now notorious in this house. Could my father have indicated that the holder of such a living would stand in need of a wife? And has Mr Worsley made application to several young ladies of his acquaintance, been turned down by them, and now makes advances to Miss Weyland?

If this is so I wonder why he was turned down. He is presentable enough, well spoken, and the living is a good one. Could it be, I wonder, that there is about him a self-centredness, a self-servingness (if there be such a word!) that suggests to them that he could be an inconsiderate, exacting husband? That, however good his principles, his own advancement will always be his paramount concern, his wife's comfort or convenience of very little moment?

If he has been rejected for that reason, it is greatly to the credit of my sex.

To turn to other matters. We have been visited by Mr James Page. To be more precise we have been visited by Mr James Page and his 'friend' Mr Fred Paisley. The latter seems to have had no contact with Mr Page since schooldays, and is as near to a total cipher as a sentient human being can well be. After a few 'How d'ye do's and an adventurous 'Lovely weather, eh?' he settled down to a fitful discussion with Amelia and

Dorothea. The conversation of a fourteen- and a thirteen-year-
old seems to be the most he is fitted for. It is well he has a
good estate, just over the border into Berkshire. Nature is kind
to nincompoops when it makes them eldest sons.

It occurs to me as I write that he may have talked to Dorothea
and Amelia *on instruction*, to free their devoted instructress.

Not, of course, that Mr Page devoted himself to Miss
Weyland. That would have been clearly improper on a visit of
courtesy to the Hudson family. Would he, in any case, have
wanted to? I am uncertain on this point. I had the impression
at times that he was – how shall I put this? – maintaining his
place in Miss Weyland's interest or affections, while at the
same time devoting himself more assiduously (alas!) to me.

'You don't find it flat, Miss Hudson, to return to the country
after the delights of London?'

'Not in the least. The delights of London as you call them
were in any case beginning to pall.'

'Really? So soon?'

'They became inextricably associated in my mind with the
noise and the constant traffic, and the bustle here and there
on silly visits that I did not want to make and the visited one
did not want to receive.'

'How exactly you sum up London!'

'Not to mention the constant babble of silly people whose
opinions are not worth listening to and whose interest one
would scorn to engage.'

'There you are surely harsh. You can hardly deny that many
of the best minds in the kingdom inhabit the metropolis.'

'Then it must somehow contrive to atrophy them, or coat
them in the same grime that clings to the buildings, the
pavements, the very trees in the parks.'

I may add, in parenthesis, that these opinions were produced
with the sole aim of being contradictory with Mr Page. I began,
in the last weeks, to be very fond of London.

'You must at least allow that, begrimed or not, some of those
buildings are splendid beyond comparison, or garlanded with
romantic associations. The Abbey, St Paul's, St James's,

Hampton Court. You must have seen many of these places –
under the guidance of your excellent instructress.'

He bowed (in a ludicrous manner, to my eyes) at Miss
Weyland, who smiled sweetly.

'We did indeed pay many such visits,' she said. 'Though
Jane has no need of guidance from me to appreciate the interest
of their past history.'

'I prefer pictures,' I said.

I give you this as a sample of our somewhat stilted
conversation. It is representative of the whole: he focused his
attention on me, with occasional conversational bobs in the
direction of Miss Weyland. By the end I was his 'dear Miss
Hudson' (without my being asked whether I wished to be!) and
it was agreed (by him!) that this was only the first of many
visits he would make while he was staying, ostensibly for the
fishing, with his cretinous friend.

Does he think I have money, do you think? Or will have at
my father's death? He is mistaken. So far as I know, at my
father's death I shall be as dependent on Andrew as I now am
on Sir Richard. Woman's destiny, to be a limpet!

(*Later*) Dr Packenham has been to see my father. He is now
closeted with Mama. I have said little to you as yet on that
score, but your letter tells me that you suspect. I realize that,
if I am right, we stand poised to gather speed as we hurtle
downhill. My father's illness constitutes some kind of lull before
the storm. (Do you hate mixed metaphors? I love them. They
are such a slap in the face for pedants!) What I mean is that
nothing can develop while my father is sick. Except that things
may develop in his *mind* – fancies, suspicions. If I were my
mother I would be even more careful than she is. When he
emerges from his sick-room, what will be his frame of mind?
What will Joseph have retailed to him? What will he have
decided to do? If, of course, he does emerge from his sick-room.

I wait in the tense, uneasy atmosphere before the first
thunder-clap.

Yours most sincerely,
Jane Hudson

A Visitor

From Sir Richard Hudson's Account Book

Item: to jewelled evening bag for Anna   £4.15/-
       to ribbons for Jane   £0.3/-
       to Miss Weyland (one month's wages)   £4.0/-
       to Joseph for his excellent work on Andrew   £0.1/-
       to Marshall's for sherry   £4.3/-

Mr James Page to Mr S. Goldstone

Dear Sammy,

But you *can't* call in the bills now. I told you when I saw you that I'd given up the gee-gees. I've given up the tables as well, and am in every respect a model citizen. I languish here at Mallerby House in Berkshire, a fine estate. I shoot, I fish, I suffer incalculable boredom, apart from the prospect of ogling a few heiresses – damned fine girls, I tell you, and *interested*. Come on, Sammy, you know that as soon as the rents come in you will get paid. You've huffed and puffed before, but never at a sillier time than this. You've always got paid in the past, and you will now. Just keep your (decidedly ugly!) nose out of my affairs and I promise by the end of the year you and I will be on an entirely different footing. But *stay your greedy hand!* You will be paid!

Yours,

J. Page

Mr James Page to Mrs Page

My dear Mama,

Please get Miss Weyland out of your head. She is becoming an obsession. I am in Berkshire, visiting a friend. No, you have not heard of this friend before. I have many friends of whom you have not heard. So please understand: I am in Berkshire, Miss Weyland is in Hampshire, or London, or Van Diemen's

Land for all I know. There are more young ladies in the world than Miss Weyland, and the more I know them the more I appreciate them.

Tell Taylor I shall want the rents on time, and no shufflings or prevarications.

Fine fishing here. Fred Paisley is the dearest chap, though no conversationalist. I shall return to Merton by the end of the month – or the beginning of August at the latest.

Meanwhile, forget Miss Weyland. I have!

Your loving son,
James

JOSEPH MORRISSEY TO MRS KATE MORRISSEY

Dear Mother,

Now I got Sir Richard in bed agane I got him right under my thum, tho he do'nt know it. He relies on me, and I do everything he tell me, only I know how to make him tell me. Three days ago I beat young Andrew so he wont sit down cumftable for a week. Enjoyed meself and got a sub from Sir Richard for good work. Well done thow good and faithfull servant so to speak. Very nice!

But what plots go on Ma! One of them I beleive I understand perfect, tho she hav'nt discused it with annyone. Of course with my power in the houshold I could prevent it. But mite'nt it profit me more not to prevent it and then milk them for everything they got? I talk of murder Ma. The power I have over Sir Richards nothing to the power Id have over a murderer who thought hed got away with it. He or she I mean. But is keeping quite too dangerous? I need you here Ma but will have to do what I thinks right.

Your perpleksed son,
Joe

A Visitor

Dear W.,

I write briefly and in haste to make you *au courant* with developments at Elmstead.

My father's renewed sickness brings Dr Packenham much to the house again. Yesterday, after seeing the invalid, he was closeted again with my mother for some time. Chancing to pass in the hall as he took his leave I found myself addressed by him: 'I have been impressing on your mother the importance of Sir Richard taking the diuretic mixture which I prescribed, and which he has given up.'

I was, I hope, sufficiently brief with him.

'I have no influence with my father. If he will not listen to you on medical matters, Dr Packenham, then to whom will he listen? Joseph, perhaps?'

He was, I know, merely excusing (unconvincingly) the fact that he had spent so long with my mother. But the idea that my father might listen to any of his womenfolk is one I had to squash. We are his pawns. But then so is Andrew. So is Mr Worsley.

À propos of which, I am sure that Miss Weyland has received a proposal of marriage, or at least some declaration of love! Yes, this latter is more likely. I saw her through the schoolroom door yesterday reading a letter that simply *must* have been a love letter. How do I know? How was she reading it? In a manner both pleased and excited (her mouth a little open), and yet with an air of some perplexity as well. I conjecture that Mr Worsley has declared himself, and she is uncertain how to respond.

To add to her uncertainty Mr James Page has again called, with his 'friend', and has behaved much as before, except that, when she was called away to supervise the girls, his behaviour to me was still more particular. Odious man! I would as soon wed his witless friend as wed him. I shall one day let him know my opinion of the male sex.

Yours sincerely,
Jane Hudson

CHAPTER NINE

The Fatal Day (I)

MISS JANE HUDSON TO AN UNIDENTIFIED
CORRESPONDENT

Dear W.,

To give an account of the day which – were I prone to the melodramatics of the lady novelists – I might call in my mind The Fatal Day will require many pages, perhaps many letters. The day's outcome you will doubtless have learned from the pages of *The Times*. Were you, perhaps, not altogether surprised? Did you wonder whether there was in the event more than *The Times* could know of – more than the death of a gentleman who for some months had been in failing health? Yes, there was indeed, but *what*, precisely, I cannot as yet say.

I must begin at the day's beginning. We sat – we of the female sorority – in the schoolroom. Amelia and Dorothea were being fractious, Miss Weyland patient but abstracted. I was apparently reading for my 'tutorial' with Mr Worsley, but in fact I was indulging in my own thoughts – about myself and my future, at times straying mentally to the related topic of Miss Weyland and her future, for in truth both our respective fates are allied, for all that my condition and my future both seem so much more hopeful than hers. We are both victims, both members of an oppressed class.

The Fatal Day (I)

I must try to put in order my thoughts about Miss Weyland.
She is sharp rather than intelligent, partially educated and
with no particular desire to improve herself in that respect. Her
mind is all on her future prospects – and who would blame
her? If Mr Worsley had shown signs of interest, not to say
empressement, when she first arrived at Elmstead Court, she
would have responded, perhaps with a wistful backwards glance
to Mr James Page, with his immeasurably better position and
fortune. (What *precisely* went on in that quarter, I wonder?) As
it is, Mr Worsley has shown his interest late, Mr James Page
is once again on the scene, and Miss Weyland is uncertain how
to respond. She may well, like me, have seen the letters in
female hands that have arrived for Mr Worsley. She weighs up
her prospects, and I for one cannot ridicule or blame her for
this.

That said, I cannot *like* her.

Dorothea and Amelia were being querulous and silly, and
pestering Miss Weyland, preventing her from thinking her
'How happy could I be with either' thoughts. Suddenly I said:

'How long will it be, do you think, before women are admitted
to universities?'

'Not in my lifetime,' said Miss Weyland.

'That is what Papa says.' (How right Papa was, for once!)
'Yet there is talk already of founding a college in London.'

'It will be a great boon,' said Miss Weyland abstractedly. I
allowed the subject to drop. But I could not take up the books
I was supposed to be reading, and sat musing on that great
tyranny, marriage. Until around half-past eleven, when Bessie
(the most irrepressible of our housemaids) put her head around
the door, her maid's cap bobbing with excitement, her eyes
sparkling.

'That Mr Page has come, an' he asked special to see Sir
Richard.'

She threw me a knowing look, but I shrugged and pretended
to return to my book.

'Joseph was sent to ask what he wanted, and now he's up in
Sir Richard's bedroom, and Lady Hudson's gone there an' all!'

Still I stayed silent, and she withdrew discontentedly.

Ten minutes later Miss Weyland said the weather had brightened, and she and her charges could have relief from their labours in a walk in the gardens. The skies seemed to me if anything to have darkened. I declined to go with them.

Andrew, Mr Worsley noticed, still took care when sitting down five days after his beating. There were, however, other changes in the boy which suggested an access of confidence and independence: he argued more fluently, he deferred less, he made suggestions to his mother with the self-assurance of one who knew he would one day be head of the household. Whether this access of confidence would survive exposure to his father's sarcasm remained to be seen. Sir Richard had kept to his room since the day of the beating, seen by none of his family except his wife, and otherwise only by Joseph and one or other of the maids. It was no secret in the house that Dr Packenham had spoken of a weakness of the heart.

'Sir Richard's attack seems as severe as any he has had,' Mr Worsley remarked as they began their morning session.

'Dr Packenham has often warned him of the dangers of over-excitement,' Andrew replied gnomically. Mr Worsley knew he should stamp down hard on such remarks, but he did not do so. Andrew, after all, might soon inherit Elmstead Court from his father. When he came of age he would have the disposal of many livings.

Their discussion of the causes of the Civil War was as lively as all discussions of that conflict tend to be. Andrew was excellent at marshalling the opposing arguments of the various historians, and showed a commendable desire to inspect the State Papers of Charles I's reign. Mr Worsley had the sensation, familiar to all teachers, of being in the presence of a mind that one day would outstrip him by far. By eleven the discussion was threatening to become circular. Andrew stretched in his desk, and then flinched.

'You feel like a walk?' Mr Worsley asked. 'It would blow away the cobwebs.'

'Yes, I think so,' said Andrew, standing up gratefully. 'Just a turn around the grounds.'

'You go on and I'll join you in ten minutes.'

Mr Worsley, in fact, felt a need to visit one of the earth closets hidden by ivy at the back of Elmstead Court. When he had satisfied his needs in one of those insalubrious but necessary places of refuge he realized that the day, though improving, was far from clement. He decided to fetch his summer scarf from the schoolroom, and instead of going over to the lawns ducked in by a back entrance. Passing down the carpeted corridor on the first floor – past Sir Richard's bedroom, past Lady Hudson's, Andrew's, the girls', to the pokey ends of the building where the schoolrooms were – he thought he heard a sound from the open doorway of his own schoolroom. He slowed down, walking carefully until he came to the doorway.

At the desk, which was open, stood Joseph. Open in his hands was the diary which Mr Worsley kept at the bottom of his pile of old schoolbooks. It was being read laboriously, finger on the line, contempt playing around his lips. When he was aware of the shadow in the doorway Joseph looked up. Far from being abashed, he leered.

'Well, well, Mr Schoolmaster! Setting traps for little Miss Weyland, are we? The 'air in the book – a very old idea. Think she's been reading the sweet nothings you've been writing about 'er, do you? Well, she 'asn't. It's been me as 'as read 'em. It's been *me* you've been wooing. 'Ow do I do as a substitute, eh? Fancy me as your sweetheart? Fancy me as the vicar's lady?'

He stood there, looming, all gross six feet of him. And there was nothing he could do: Joseph was Sir Richard's favourite, perhaps his emissary. He was inviolate.

Mr Worsley wheeled round and strode back along the corridor.

LADY HUDSON TO DR PACKENHAM

Lady Hudson begs Dr Packenham, if he can make it convenient, to call at Elmstead Court in the course of the afternoon. Though Sir Richard's condition has certainly not markedly deteriorated, his symptoms give some cause for alarm which his wife is anxious to have allayed.

Joseph, who will bear this, can give Dr Packenham details of these symptoms, since he has been in constant attendance on Sir Richard.

Gratefully,

Lady Hudson

Mr James Page emerged from Sir Richard's bedroom dissatisfied. Not with himself – he was a young man who was never that. On the other hand he was frequently dissatisfied with other people when they failed to live up to the obligations which he thought they had towards himself. Even his heavy losses on the horses and at the tables he attributed to a malign Fate – personalized into a figure not unlike his dead father – which had denied him the win which he had a right to expect on every bet and every hand of cards. Even his good fortune, such as his early inheritance of Merton Hall and a substantial fortune with it, he put down merely to his just deserts. And that was three years in the past. Certainly he had had very little good fortune lately.

Now he indulged in irritable thoughts about Sir Richard Hudson. Why couldn't the man speak out clearly? Why couldn't he – not to put too fine a point on it – name a sum?

He was half conscious that when he had talked of the warmth of his regard for Sir Richard's eldest daughter his ardour had somehow not rung true – had sounded hollow or forced. He was used to wooing young women – had had some notable successes in that line, as one person in that very house could have testified if she would – but he was quite unused to talking about them to their fathers. And what a damnably foolish position it put a man into, this asking permission of the father to seek the daughter's hand, when he had no idea (beyond a definite sense of the charms of his person and his estate) whether she would accept him or not. Yes – a damnably foolish position, made worse by the difficulty of bringing the subject round at this early stage to the question of money.

Sir Richard had been friendly and expansive, as far as his enfeebled state had permitted. He had uttered admiring noises during James's account (with significant omissions) of his estate, wealth, and position in the county of Norfolk. In the subsequent conversation he had made encouraging remarks such as 'The man who marries Jane will never be a pauper,' and 'Fortunately I have it in my power to do something handsome for Jane.' But he had never committed the vulgarity of putting a figure to what he would do. How a little vulgarity would have improved matters!

And when he came to think things over, just how encouraging had Sir Richard's remarks been? To say that he had it in his power to do something handsome for Jane did not amount to a promise actually to do it. How much better if Sir Richard had not had it in his power to *withhold* a fortune with Jane's hand – if she had inherited a pretty sum from some doting grandparent such as the northern mill-owner he had heard about. And when he said that the man who married Jane would never be a pauper he could have meant – My God! Could he have heard? Could he have got some inkling? Could Sammy—?

No, Sammy was as safe as the Bank of England. Had to be – because on that the power of his threats depended. On the other hand the gentlemen of the turf, the card-playing partners at Boodles and White's . . . But if he had heard, why would Sir Richard be so welcoming, so encouraging? No, for sure he had not heard.

And James was sure that Sammy's hand would be stayed by the mere rumour that he was to marry an heiress. The mere bruiting of it abroad would give him time – that desperately needed time. Then, if matters of finance proved unsatisfactory, the whole matter could be dropped, no announcement having been made. Sir Richard had been described to him by a race-course acquaintance as 'rich as Croesus', but that could have been one of the commonplaces of the turf. And to be rich was not necessarily to be generous. Well – if he were to prove close-fisted, that was the end of it. His only desire – in matters amorous, as in all other things – was to amuse himself as best pleased him. As he had with Frances Weyland. And as he fully intended to go on doing after marriage.

His brow clearing, he passed through the heavy portals of Elmstead Court and out into the watery sun.

Under the line of elms at the end of the lawns, where they began to slope as rough grassland down to the river, Andrew Hudson and Mr Worsley were walking in silence. Andrew had observed his tutor's preoccupation when he had joined him, and had even ventured to enquire what was troubling him. Mr Worsley merely shook his head and said it was 'nothing of moment'. Andrew was quite content to walk in silence, having matters to think about himself.

It was Andrew who observed James Page emerging from the house, but his noticing it caused Mr Worsley to cease his moody walking and observe it too. It's like watching a stage play, thought Andrew, who had been interested in the motives behind the young man's visits. They saw Mr Page start towards the group of three on the lawn: Miss Weyland and her two younger charges. Then they saw him swerve aside as his eye was caught by a bonnet to be seen over the hedges around the rose garden – the bonnet of Jane Hudson.

In that moment Mr Worsley made a decision.

As he rode towards Elmstead and Dr Packenham's residence, Joseph was thinking furiously. When he had got back from the schoolroom to Sir Richard's bedroom his master was asleep but Lady Hudson was still there, and had been since Mr Page's visit. She had professed to see in Sir Richard's sleeping some cause for anxiety, and Joseph, though he knew his master often slept during the day, had agreed with her. Often in the past he had resisted leaving Sir Richard and Lady Hudson alone, knowing that she hated him and resented his influence. Today, seeing in his mistress a repressed agitation that could not be accounted for by Mr Page's visit, he had gone willingly.

Today might be *the* day.

MISS JANE HUDSON TO AN UNIDENTIFIED CORRESPONDENT (CONTINUED)

You will ask what possessed me to go out into the grounds without first ascertaining from Pennywear or one of the maids whether Mr James Page had left the house. In truth I cannot imagine. I can only think that I was lost in my thoughts – on subjects such as those that we talked over on our two meetings – and simply forgot Bessie's news and her sly innuendo. Suffice it to say that, when I saw the sun shining I decided to go out without a qualm of doubt, and as I went past my father's bedroom I heard him talking and assumed it was to Joseph. Though we knew he was sick and incommunicado to most of the family (not that we desired to be communicado!), Joseph was always with him, and was talked to as freely as if he were the family's legal man, or my father's spiritual adviser.

I left the house by a side door. I knew Miss Weyland and my sisters were on the lawns, and I wanted to avoid their notice as I had no desire to be called over to join them. (Not that Miss Weyland is in any way intrusive or over-familiar. I am determined to do justice to her. She is torn between two men with very different prospects, and she is weighing up where her self-interest lies. Such a calculation is one that a woman in a position such as hers *must make.* I might add that it is my father's belief that this is the calculation that everyone invariably makes.)

To cut my account short, I gained the rose garden, and there could walk in peace, enjoying the fine displays and thinking my thoughts. I have observed to you before that I have a sense of things somehow hurtling towards a climax, a disaster, or at the very least a turning-point. It was of this feeling that I was thinking, trying to analyse what gave me the idea. I had been in the rose garden barely ten minutes, however, when to my horror I saw Mr James Page approaching across the lawn.

You will not think I make any great claims to perception when I say that I knew at once what was in the wind. What is a woman's life but birth, marriage, and death? I had gone through the first, do not soon anticipate the last, so what remains? A man approaching a woman may be intent on uttering witless nothings (usually is) or he may be making moves towards seduction or matrimony. There was a purpose in Mr Page's step that told in favour of matrimony.

In a minute or two the puppy was before me, all smiles and insouciant charm.

'Miss Hudson, what a beautiful day!'

'The weather has certainly cleared somewhat,' I said, continuing my walk.

'I am so glad to find you alone.'

'Oh?'

It was said with the intention of freezing him utterly, and no doubt if I had had more experience – the experience that being properly 'out' in London society would give, the experience of puppies and their ways – I could have done it convincingly and effectively. As it was he remained unfrozen.

'Yes, indeed. I have just come from talking to your father.'

'Really? Papa is denied us at the moment, due to the severity of his current attack. No doubt he feels that the stimulus of male company and conversation is just what he needs.'

Sarcasm passed entirely over his head. He walked along beside me smiling with ineffable self-conceit, nodding, as if to say that this was doubtless my father's feeling. It is clear that Mr James Page thinks himself equal to the wisest and most articulate statesman in Christendom.

'When I say I have been talking to your Papa, I mean that I have been talking on a particular subject.'

'Most sensible people do.'

'The particular subject – as I am sure a young lady of your perception does not need to be told – of you, Miss Hudson.'

I greeted the news with total silence. A sensible man would have understood that silence. Mr Page talked on.

The Fatal Day (I)

'Miss Hudson, I'm sure you cannot have been unaware that ever since that memorable night at the opera I have been – I have had – had a most especial interest in you. That was – I will make no disguise of the matter – the motive for renewing my friendship with Fred Paisley, and for soliciting from him an invitation to visit him at his home.'

'Really?' I said, with the utmost coolness. 'I rather imagined – if I thought about the matter at all – that your acquaintanceship with Miss Weyland must have been the cause.'

'Oh come, Miss Hudson! Miss Weyland is a gov— Miss Weyland is the friend of my sister, and no more to me than – than my sister's maid. No, my dear Miss Hudson, I was most powerfully attracted to Hampshire and the vicinity of Elmstead Court by *you*, and I may say that as we have become better acquainted in the course of my visit, I have been most strikingly struck – most strikingly impressed by the charms of your person, as well as the strength of your – of your *mind* – that would not be too strong a word – and so powerful is the impression you have made on my heart that I felt impelled to solicit an interview with your father, so that I might make him aware of my hopes.'

Mr Page, you will note, gets the language of his proposal from bad novels. Certain it is that his words were not winged by the strength of any personal feeling!

'And Papa? Did he tell you that I am only eighteen, and hardly ready to be put on the marriage market?'

'I am happy to say he did not. He was, I may say, most encouraging. But let us forget your father, dear Miss Hudson. What I am here to solicit is your *own* good opinion. I have to plead my cause several of what the world calls advantages: a considerable estate, a position in the world in spite of my youth, a family of an excellent mother and sisters who would I know love you as they love each other. But I believe that what will really plead my cause is the strength of the attraction you exert over me, the feelings—'

It was time to put an end to his burblings.

'Mr Page, I am gratified that you find me attractive, but

desolated to have to tell you that I, on the contrary, find you anything but attractive. My answer to the question which you have not yet got around to asking is no. And if you retain any wish to please me you will leave the home of your cretinous friend and put as great a distance between us as possible.'

I could have turned and made for the shelter of the house, but I preferred to outface him. After looking at me with incredulity and stuttering a few broken words, he turned and ran from me, seeking the comforts of the stables and a retreat on horseback from his discomfiture.

CHAPTER TEN

The Fatal Day (II)

Sir Richard's bedroom was the largest in Elmstead Court, but it abutted a disused, poky bedroom at the corner of the house that overlooked the lawns on one side, the shrubbery on the other. When Sir Richard's attacks became a regular feature of his life it was found that the little dressing room between his and Lady Hudson's bedroom was too small for Joseph, the medicines, and the aids to locomotion that had become necessary. Workmen from the estate were called in to make a door between the poky bedroom and Sir Richard's rather grand one, and Joseph established himself there in some style, always on call and yet essentially private. He regarded it and treated it as his room, a space on which he could set his mark. Here he was removed from the essentially communal life below stairs. Here he wrote his little notes to his mother. Here he thought. Here he contrived.

Mr Worsley and Miss Weyland were perfectly aware of this fact, but they forgot to take it into account on the afternoon of Sir Richard's death. Perhaps Mr Worsley's upsetting experience of the morning accounted for this in his case, and perhaps her perplexity as to what to answer accounted for it in Miss Weyland's. However that may be, the fact was that he chose the shrubbery to make the first advances on what might sentimentally be termed Miss Weyland's heart, and that these advances were overheard. They were walking up and down along the paths under the window, and Mr Worsley's voice and even his walk were becoming just a shade parsonical.

79

'I have had to contemplate for some time,' he said in tones that were rather more than casual, 'the prospect that my time at Elmstead Court is limited. My charge will, I hope, go up to Cambridge, and then my work here will be at an end.'

'He will do great credit to you wherever he goes,' said Miss Weyland earnestly.

'Not *dis*credit, at any rate, I hope.'

'My own time here,' said Miss Weyland, willing to reply in kind, 'may not be as long as it seemed in prospect. Jane is now a woman, and it cannot be denied that her sisters, though charming girls, do not have her powers of mind. It may well be that Lady Hudson will not decide to continue their education beyond the next year or two.'

Mr Worsley cast his eyes in the air.

'Education! Sometimes I wonder about the usefulness of our profession. What do we do that cannot be better done by an enquiring mind let loose in a good library?'

'Your opinion is biased,' said Miss Weyland, with the tiniest touch of tartness, 'by having a pupil with an enquiring mind. What use is a good library to an *un*enquiring mind?'

Mr Worsley thought that a surprisingly good point.

'True, true. But – biased as you rightly say that I am – my experience with Andrew predisposes me to a change of course. Any pupil after him will be a disappointment, an anti-climax. Which brings me to something I have been seeking an opportunity of opening to you, Miss Weyland, for some time.'

Upstairs Joseph ran, surprisingly light-footed, to the door which led to Sir Richard's bedroom.

'If I'm not mistaken,' he said, his voice low, 'Mr Worsley is screwing 'imself up, so to speak, to a proposal.'

Joseph could imagine rather than see the strained lips across the teeth that constituted Sir Richard's smile on such occasions.

'More fool he,' he heard from the bed.

'Time for your medicine,' said Joseph. 'Sir.'

*

Andrew, enjoying an unexpected furlough when he would normally have been reading Horace or Virgil, walked down the sloping wilderness towards the river – one of the loveliest places in the grounds of Elmstead Court, and one of the loneliest. It was his favourite spot for meditation.

It was coming to Andrew, as it had come to Jane, that events at Elmstead Court were reaching some kind of crisis. He had a similar sense of an unstoppable progress, as of a cart hurtling downhill. It was the same sense he had got when a beating had become inevitable.

This time his sense of events rolling forward out of control sprang from his father's illness. His attacks had never been so severe or so long-lasting, his contact with his family never so completely severed. No intimation of improvement had reached his children – on the contrary, their mother had been more abstracted than ever, and had responded to any enquiries (mostly from Mr Worsley or Miss Weyland) with sighs and shakes of the head. It occurred to Andrew that this was not the only development that seemed to forebode change or disaster: something about his mother also contributed to his sense of events rolling out of control, though he was unable to pin down what it was.

The pain of his last beating had almost left him, but the memory had not. That memory was not just of pain, but of humiliation. There was no oblivion, no forgiveness for his father: his enjoyment of such occasions was now clear, and a hard ridge of hatred had formed in his mind. He had never liked his father, never felt easy in his presence. Now he not only hated him but also despised him.

He faced the crux of the matter briefly in his mind: he would be glad if his father died. That matter faced, contemplated honestly, he put it from his mind and went on to other things.

What he needed above all was to consult the family solicitor. He could certainly find some excuse for going with Mr Worsley into Marwick, one of the nearby towns, where the solicitor had his office. But what excuse could he give his tutor for visiting Mr Winterburn? And would old Winterburn see him, answer his

81

questions, even granted that he must know the state of his father's health? Would he see him even if his father were dead, in view of the fact that he would still be a minor?

Yes, Andrew rather thought: if his father was dead, Mr Winterburn would tell him what he wanted to know, even though he would still be a minor.

'The situation is such,' said Mr Worsley, after providing a cool résumé of the matter which omitted any mention of Sir Richard's stipulation of marriage, 'that I must think seriously about the duties and responsibilities of a country clergyman.'

'Such a position is only to be entered into after mature consideration,' agreed Miss Weyland.

'And any such consideration includes, inevitably, the question of the clergyman's wife.'

'Yes, indeed,' responded Miss Weyland, primly neutral. Her mind, however, was racing. Such an opening could only lead in one direction. What had James Page's interview with Jane in the rose garden that morning meant? What had been behind his hurried and undignified departure? Did that mean there was still a chance in that direction? If not, here was a chance. And Miss Weyland was, in spite of her loftier hopes and ambitions, a realist, and determined not to throw away a chance. Any chance.

'I have given great thought,' went on Mr Worsley, still walking in a clerical manner, hands clasped behind his back, 'to the sort of role a parson's wife must play in the life of a small country community, and the sort of qualities such a role calls for.'

'Everyone must have thought of such things – everyone who has lived in such a community and seen the possibilities for good and harm.'

If Miss Weyland spoke unusually warmly it was with the memory of the country clergyman and his wife in the small village where her own father had died. The main concern of that pair had been that her bereft and hard-pressed family should be got out of the neighbourhood and found to be someone else's responsibility as quickly as decency permitted. It was a bitter memory.

'Ah,' said Mr Worsley, breaking in on her reverie. 'You *have* given thought to the problems of occupying such a position. May I ask what your conclusions were?'

Miss Weyland thought fast.

'Conclusions is much too grand a word for any such poor and scattered thoughts as mine,' she said slowly. 'I have merely seen it as inevitable that the clergyman – the parson – must try to engage his parishioners on the theoretical level – must put to them the moral and religious considerations that should engage every Christian soul, putting them to his flock abstractly. Whereas his wife must engage herself both by example and precept on the practical level, giving counsel, giving practical aid – illustrating, in fact, true Christianity at work.'

'Admirable!' breathed Mr Worsley, as if he had just been soaking up the wisdom of a Pusey or a Newman.

Upstairs in Sir Richard's suite of rooms Joseph again darted to the connecting door.

'Working round to it nicely,' he commented in his coarse voice. 'Both of 'em finding out where their interests lie. We'll have that second proposal, you mark my words, Sir Richard.'

Sir Richard, on the bed, merely grunted.

Down in the shrubbery Mr Worsley, who had a fair idea of what had happened in the rose garden that morning, was in something of the same mind. Two proposals at Elmstead Court in one day! '*La Folle Journée*,' he said to himself, in impeccable French.

But something in that thought reined him in. Irrevocable steps were not in his nature. There was no hurry. There was perhaps everything to lose from hurry.

'I think you understand which way this conversation has been going,' he said, with apparent urgency.

Frances Weyland merely looked modestly at the path.

'On the other hand, with Sir Richard in his present condition, it would seem unfeeling and inappropriate if we came to any binding decision now.'

Miss Weyland was unable to decide whether it was relief or disappointment that swept through her.

'You think Sir Richard is seriously ill?'

'I do. I base my fears on Lady Hudson's demeanour and her replies to questions. I believe that she is very worried.'

'In that case, Mr Worsley—'

'William. Please call me William when we are alone.'

'William. In that case it would indeed be unfeeling to be thinking of our own affairs.'

'Exactly my opinion. Though *think* of them we must. But let us consider privately our views and feelings. Let us get to know each other still better. But let us reach no final decision until we have better news of Sir Richard.'

'No indeed. Or—'

Mr Worsley put his finger to his lips.

Upstairs Joseph went back into his master's bedroom.

'He's backed off – shied at the starting post. Thinks it would be unfeeling in your present condition.'

He gave a coarse laugh. From the bed there came another grunt, then something louder. As Joseph hurried to the bed his master lolled to one side and vomited.

'Oh dear, oh dear,' said Joseph. 'That's not very nice, is it?'

Miss Jane Hudson to an Unidentified Correspondent (continued)

In short, the result of my morning's work with Mr James Page is that I feel I have become a woman – by not choosing *that* way of becoming a woman. The way, that is, that most of my sex are forced or persuaded into. I do not rely on your agreeing with me in general, though in this particular case I am sure you will. I merely tell you that the experience confirmed me in my conviction that I am destined for something other than marriage and children.

The consequences of this conviction, I believe, are that I must get myself educated to the highest level possible for a woman in this 'enlightened' age. The openings for this are as yet unclear in my mind, but they certainly are limited. You, with your metropolitan upbringing, will know more than I do. Perhaps the truth is that I must educate myself.

When Lady Hudson came into Sir Richard's sickroom in the middle of the afternoon she nodded to Joseph and bustled straight over to the bed. He followed behind her, his manner different from that he assumed towards Sir Richard, but far from obsequious.

'He's thrown up once or twice, Your Ladyship,' he said, in his footman's voice. 'I've been very worried.'

Lady Hudson looked at her husband, who was either sleeping or for some other reason not registering her presence.

'And Dr Packenham hasn't been? No, of course he would have come to see me.'

'Of course, Your Ladyship.'

'How long is it since he last vomited?'

'About a quarter of an hour, Your Ladyship.'

'Has he spoken since?' Her manner was becoming more perturbed, and she wrung her hands.

'Nothing what you'd call coherent, Your Ladyship. Just odd words I couldn't rightly make out.'

'God in heaven!' murmured Lady Hudson. 'You should have sent word.'

She bustled over to a chest of drawers under the window, on which stood a quill and a bottle of ink. She took a small sheet of paper with the Hudson arms on it and wrote: 'Come quickly. Sir Richard's condition is deteriorating.' She blotted it, folded the note, then hurried back to Joseph.

'Take this to Dr Packenham. Take a hunter and find him out wherever he is.'

Joseph bent his head and went to the door. There he summoned by a glance the skivvy whom he had earlier placed on the landing, and whispered to her in the doorway. He handed over the folded sheet, and shifted his bulk back into Sir Richard's bedroom. From the bed Lady Hudson looked at him with raised eyebrows.

'I sent Edward, Your Ladyship, as being the better horseman,' he said.

She looked him straight in the eyes, and he gazed back in a parody of respect. The trial of strength between them was cut short by a strangled grunt from the bed. Lady Hudson turned at once and bent over it.

'Yes, dear? Richard . . . ?'

The voice when it came was indistinct.

'That puppy . . . James Something . . . Has he gone?'

Lady Hudson frowned, mystified.

'Mr Page? Oh yes, I believe he left about midday, in something of a hurry. I don't know how much he said to Jane. Why, Richard?'

'Send Jane to me—'

The voice slurred away and the eyes closed. The breathing became more stertorous. Lady Hudson straightened, but paused by the bed, uncertain what to do.

'I suppose we'd better . . . though it doesn't seem as though he'll be able to talk to her.' She turned to Joseph. 'Yes, we must. Will you go and bring Miss Jane, Joseph? Go yourself this time, please.'

Joseph went reluctantly to the door, looked around suspiciously, and then was heard to hurry along the corridor. When he returned Lady Hudson was still by the bed, bending most solicitously over the form of her husband. Joseph shot her a glance, then closed the door and stood by it, impassively watching the bed.

Mr William Worsley was writing in his diary.

The thought strikes me that I am a fortunate man, or like to be one. Miss Weyland is intelligent, right-thinking, attractive, and with an excellent manner. As a clergyman's wife she would be exemplary, and as my own helpmeet everything that I could ask for. I must now hope and pray that Sir Richard's health improves, so that we may bring affairs to a head. I pray to God for his improvement, but today no good report has come from the sickroom.

Mr Worsley wiped his pen and ended the entry. He closed the book thoughtfully and stood for a moment irresolute. Now that he knew Joseph rather than Miss Weyland was the reader of his intimate thoughts, or rather his feigned thoughts, he could no longer keep the diary in his desk. There was also now no reason to overstate Miss Weyland's charm or intelligence, but he was conscious of having done so. It was, in fact, in the nature of an insurance – should the diary be found by his wife after marriage, for instance.

He pondered where to put the book. It was too large to keep on his person. Finally he went up to his bedroom on the second floor and locked it in the trunk which he had brought to Elmstead Court five years earlier, with the meagre relics of his early life and his hopes and ambitions for the future.

Pausing for a moment to look out of the window he saw approaching at great speed on horseback the figure of Dr Packenham. Mr Worsley hurried downstairs again.

With Jane Hudson's fetching from the schoolroom to her father's sick-bed, all pretence of the house following its normal routine was abandoned. Jane had been reading aloud to her sisters a rather elementary book about India and its inhabitants which Andrew had handed on to her when the skivvy burst in with her summons – the frightened girl only sure that Miss Jane was to go, incoherent otherwise as to the reasons. When Jane rose silently and went out into the corridor her sisters followed her at a distance. After a moment's thought Miss Weyland went with them. They stood, silent and apprehensive, some doors down from Sir Richard's bedroom. When, some minutes later, Andrew came in from the grounds he went up to them and whispered questions as to what had occurred. When he had heard what little they could tell him he left the group and stationed himself nearer the bedroom door.

None of them knew what they expected, though Andrew at least knew what he hoped.

In the bedroom Lady Hudson and Joseph waited for Dr Packenham, he watching her and she, more covertly, watching him. The figure on the bed gave occasional signs of life, in the form of grunts, or vain, half-conscious attempts to vomit. Then both pairs of eyes turned to the bed, soon to resume their watch on each other. When Jane knocked on the door Lady Hudson said 'Come in,' in a small, uncertain voice, and Jane walked in and stood at the foot of the bed, looking at her father composedly.

'I don't know if . . .' Lady Hudson began, uncertainly. 'I'm afraid it was something to do with Mr Page, dear. He asked for you.'

'How long ago, Mother?'

'About five minutes. When he was last . . . conscious.'

Jane thought for a moment, and then advanced down the side of the great bed.

'You wanted to speak to me, Papa?'

A nerve flickered in the forehead, then an eyelid opened. Jane felt her heart beat as she waited. Another second, then the other eye painfully opened.

'Jane?'

The voice seemed to come from a deep pit.

'Yes, Papa?'

'Mr James P – P—'

'Mr Page has gone, Papa.'

'I have . . . decided . . . you will m – m—'

Jane was silent.

'I order you . . . you to . . . to m—'

Jane meditated a statement of intent – a declaration that she had no intention of marrying at anyone's behest. Then she looked at the hideous, straining face, from which the words were forced like the rocks thrown up in 'Kubla Khan'. This man was straining to produce that scene of parental tyranny which he had planned for her, but he was dying to produce it. I have no need to make gestures to a dying man, Jane thought proudly. I will save my strength for worthier causes, more equal fights. Meanwhile she waited by the bed as the words spluttered into silence.

The Fatal Day (II)

A new sound invaded that silence – the sound of booted feet hurrying up the stairs. The watchers on the landing outside were still more conscious of it, and stepped back to the wall as Dr Packenham, as near running as any respectable medical practitioner could be, hastened to Sir Richard's bedroom, his face set in a mask of extreme anxiety. On his entrance Jane drew back from the bed, to take up a position to the right of the bed, down from her mother, while Dr Packenham immediately sat down on the bed to the patient's left. The grunting noises were continuing, and suddenly there was another attempt at vomiting. Dr Packenham spoke his patient's name urgently, then again, felt his brow and pulse, then put his face close to his open mouth and smelt his breath. As Sir Richard let out a last grunt and lay back with a great expelling of breath Jane saw Dr Packenham turn his face to her mother with a terrible look of horror and accusation.

CHAPTER ELEVEN

The Funeral

JOSEPH MORRISSEY TO MRS KATE MORRISSEY

Dear Mother,
Youv got to come here mother. I need your help bad. Hes
gone and its my betting it was'nt natral. I talked to Mrs Turner
in the village she keeps a small shop and does the post and
things, she has a room. She could acept help in the shop in
lew. Come as soon as you can as I need your advis if Im going
to get them under my thum as I plan to, you showed me how
ma, remember? Keep quite as to who you are, as will Mrs
Turner.

Your loving son,
Joe

LADY HUDSON TO THE HONOURABLE MRS WALTON-
SMITH

Dearest Mama,
The funeral is over! Oh, the tears I have shed these past
days! Every post brings letters, first from our excellent

neighbours here in the County, more recently from London and the *whole country*, all testifying to the high regard Richard was held in by statesmen and common people alike, and all arousing in his desolate widow emotions that can *only* find expression in *floods of tears*. They speak of loss – of loss to the district, loss to the country. But what is such a loss to mine – of the most excellent, generous husband and affectionate father to his children?

At first nothing could exceed my prostration of grief, and I could not be persuaded to leave the *fatal chamber* where my darling lay. My only wish was to be left alone with the remains of him who for twenty and more years had been the dearest thing on earth to me. At length, in extremes of weeping, I allowed myself to be supported by Jane to my own bedroom, where I could indulge myself unseen in my sorrow. Dr Packenham, I believe, supervised the sickroom and the *mournful rites of death*. Excellent man! By the next day I was sufficiently recovered – I had need to be, for the sake of my bereft children! – to receive him in the drawing room, where he assured Jane and Andrew and me that the melancholy outcome of Richard's illness was one which he had foreseen as a possibility, though he had most strenuously fought to ward it off. Dear Richard's own disinclination to accept medical advice and treatment – which we had treated at times almost as a joke, though I had fought against it – must have rendered his untimely end yet more likely. As Dr Packenham judiciously observed, his neighbours and friends must have *hoped* for a different outcome to his sufferings, but they cannot have *expected* one.

The funeral, dear Mama, was most affecting, as you would have felt yourself most keenly had your own infirmities allowed you to leave Brighton. The attendance – not the *empty* show of carriages, but *attendance* – was most gratifying, or would have been had I been in a state of mind to feel anything but the most terrible sense of my loss. Suffice it to say that the Earl of Eastland was present, and, though the foremost, he was surrounded by others who were scarcely his inferiors in the eyes of the world. The church at Elmstead village was *full*, and

many humble men and women – beneficiaries, no doubt, of
Richard's excellent understanding of the charitable role that a
country gentleman should play in the community – waited in
the churchyard to pay their respects. The vicar of Elmstead
was assisted in the service by the rector of Little Burdock –
poor old Mr Harmsworth! Far from well himself, indeed failing,
yet anxious to play his part in the last melancholy tributes to
Richard.

'Sir Richard Hudson was a man of wealth and standing, yet
one who in exercising power and patronage was always fair
and judicious. A charitable neighbour, a generous employer, a
loving husband, and indulgent father – to see such virtues
brought to an early grave amid universal sorrow is indeed to
drink the cup of mortality to its bitterest dregs.'

I asked the vicar to copy out those words from his address,
as I knew you would be struck by them. I remember, dearest
Mama, how your early opposition to Richard's suit – from your
feeling that his family origins were too humble – was overcome
by his firm persistence, and by your growing appreciation of
the force and worth of his sterling nature. It was indeed his
determination that won you over, as it carried the day against
all opposition, until the sad enfeeblement of his last days.

And now I must fill his place! Yet how impossible that is to
do! The decisions that he would have taken, I must take; the
courses of action he would have laid down, I must somehow
puzzle out. On whom am I to depend? I cannot expect Dr
Packenham – *worthy* man though he is in *every way* – to run to
my side to give advice at every perplexity. Lawyers may – in
their own good time! – give advice, but they can hardly
determine the course of action in family matters which (young
as the children still are, much too young to make their own
decisions) will frequently call for decisions in the future. I am
so alone, and I feel it so keenly!

Meanwhile I rely in everyday matters on the excellent
common sense of Pennywear. I sometimes thought that after
his many years in our service he rather resented the reliance
that Richard placed on Joseph, his man. No doubt it was

Richard's physical infirmities that led to this – a strong right
arm was more use to him than the sterling sense and wide
experience of an elderly butler. Nevertheless I shall not continue
this course of action. I have made it clear to Pennywear how
deeply I value his devotion, and what a high value I set on his
judgement. As to Joseph, I pay tribute to his *Trojan* work
during Richard's last illness and before: it may be that some
pecuniary acknowledgement may be appropriate. Beyond that
he must find his own level and his own means of being useful.
Any suggestion of his not knowing his place must be stamped
upon vigorously.

So now, mournfully, I face a *bereft* future, knowing that in
the years to come my role is as a MOTHER, no longer as a *wife*.
In time to come, no doubt, I shall rely on my two eldest
children, for Jane and Andrew both have qualities of mind –
though *very* different – which will assure them of an honoured
place in society, as well as ensure that they are useful to their
mother. But in the course of time, and probably *soon*, Jane will
marry, and Andrew must be allowed to test his wings in the
wider world. Richard's wonderful strength of character meant
that Andrew was sometimes undervalued. You have remarked
yourself that Richard seemed at times to take a sarcastic and
dismissive attitude to the boy. Amelia and Dorothea, on the
other hand, are essentially frivolous – something that must be
checked and curbed, but which will never be eradicated. They
will never be companions for their mother. I see myself in the
years ahead as ALONE, and pray to God to grant me the wisdom
and judgement to make right decisions.

And now, dearest Mama, I must end this second letter to
you as a WIDOW. If only Dr Packenham were to recommend
for the family the recuperative powers of sea air! But I fear that
even if he did we could not at present absent ourselves from
Elmstead Court, and the *burden* of cares and affairs that presses on
us, and particularly ME, at this melancholy time. But be assured
that at the earliest time possible you will receive a visit from

your bereaved but loving daughter,

Anna

*

MISS JANE HUDSON TO AN UNIDENTIFIED
CORRESPONDENT

Dear W.,

Well! The mummery of the funeral is over! It was got through
with all the usual trappings: the County came in moderate
numbers, the family feigned a more than respectable degree of
grief, and the clergy lied about his virtues. The rector of Little
Burdock insisted on assisting, and there was something ineffably
droll in watching his bumblings and fumblings, knowing that
Papa was (I'm fairly sure) intending to get rid of him precisely
because he could no longer tolerate his inefficiency.

It strikes me that, in that at least, we are alike: we neither
of us can stand incompetence.

And now, the mummery over (and I can see the point of the
mummery, for it marks most decisively an *end*) I must get on
with my own life, or *start* it. In some ways I regret the opposition
that my father would have represented: his will against mine
would have been as a testing of steel. Mama presents no such
challenge.

That does not mean that my future course will be easily set
or taken. If I went to her in her drawing room and said:
'Mama, I have decided that marriage and children are not for
me, and that I shall devote myself to the education and
advancement of my sex,' Mama would probably say 'Have
another piece of cake, my dear,' and change the subject. She
is already contemplating further visits to London, no doubt,
where she will arrange that I be introduced to more prospective
husbands. The former I shall accept (for London, I see now,
unlike Oxford and Cambridge, represents for women prospects
of education and enlightenment), while the latter I shall reject
– no doubt in large numbers over the years if my mother has
her way, and until she understands that I will not be forced
into the slavery of marriage.

For we differ fundamentally, my mother and I: she is a
woman whose life has revolved around men (or rather, until
recently at least, around one man), whereas I intend my life to

revolve around the female sex in general – to right wrongs, and to open up vistas unimagined by women of my mother's generation.

Meanwhile I am troubled by a certain indecisiveness in Mama. She should be seizing the reins of power and asserting her authority, but she is not doing so. Perhaps this is because she is unable to escape from the pattern of (at least superficial) deference which my father's authoritarian disposition laid down for her. Yet I am haunted by the fear that it is connected to the look I saw Dr Packenham give her as my father died.

CHAPTER TWELVE

A Family in Mourning

The events of the fatal day and the days succeeding it were on the surface very much as they were described in Lady Hudson's letter to her mother (the hard-faced relict of a cold, supercilious man, and the terror of other such in Brighton). However, the objective observer might have put a different gloss on some of the events, and there were other happenings which Lady Hudson did not see fit to mention, and others still that she neither saw nor, for a time, heard of.

The lady's grief over her husband's corpse and her extreme reluctance to leave it were something of a surprise to many of the people in the death chamber, including her two eldest children: she had not the reputation with them of a warm-hearted woman, or an emotional one. It occurred to her daughter Jane that her mother wished above all things to be left alone in the room, but could think of no convincing excuse to give that might bring this about. When finally she let herself be led away the keen eye (and Joseph, for one, was watching with a very keen eye) might have detected a pleading look cast in the direction of Dr Packenham. The worthy doctor immediately took charge. He wrote a brief note on the chest of drawers, sealed it, and then handed it to Joseph.

'See that this is taken to Parsons, the undertaker. Perhaps it would be best if you were to take it yourself. I have things to do in this room – melancholy things – which only I can perform.'

Joseph was visibly reluctant, but he had now no power base on which to rely when he wanted to disobey orders. He bowed and withdrew, though only on to the landing outside, for he had no intention of fulfilling the errand himself. It was while he was talking to Edward Harkness, one of the grooms, that he heard the key turn softly in the lock of Sir Richard's bedroom. A minute later he heard the same noise from the door of the little bedroom he had adopted as his own. He noted these things down on his mental list of interesting facts, but inwardly he chafed at his own reduced power both to observe events and to influence them.

Once he was alone and beyond the danger of any embarrassing interruption, Dr Packenham performed the necessary rites with a haste that went beyond the perfunctory, a haste which in normal circumstances he would not have shown to the merest pauper. Then he stood in the centre of the room and looked around it. He ran to the chest on which the many medicaments he had prescribed for Sir Richard stood, cast a rapid eye over them, sniffed at one or two, and shook his head. Then he knelt down and opened every drawer, feeling hastily into the back of each of them. Muttering a curse he looked under the bed, into the two wardrobes, peering at the floors, feeling into the pockets of jackets and coats, finally standing on a chair to look on top. Round the room he went again, and then again, never bothering to go into Joseph's sanctum (certainly it would not have been put in *there*), but covering the bedroom and the little dressing room as thoroughly as his haste would allow. When he felt he could not in all conscience delay any longer without arousing suspicion he left the room in a stately fashion, locked the door of the bedroom, and delivered the key to Lady Hudson's maid at the door to her bedroom.

'The undertaker and his assistant will be here by evening,' he said in his well-practised hushed tones. 'No doubt it will be best to say nothing to her ladyship of them.' Then he made a stately exit from Elmstead which was quite at odds with the inner turmoil that was racking him.

It was not till much later – not till night, in fact – that Joseph gained unimpeded access to Sir Richard's bedroom. He had, of course, a key, but he had had to let the undertaker hold sway for much of the evening. When, around midnight, he finally let himself in, he first put a light by the coffin, then placed a chair by it. That done, he began a search which was in essence very like that undertaken by Dr Packenham. When he had checked the same places with the same results – though he took longer, for he was less sure what he was looking for – he stood in the centre of the room, wondering where to try next. Suddenly a thought struck him: surely she could not have known of Sir Richard's 'secret' hidey-hole? Where he kept his books that were of a nature that Joseph, laboriously spelling through them, could barely understand, not to mention the letters from ladies in London who were certainly not such as would be received in the drawing room of his wife?

He walked over to the most capacious of the wardrobes, and with a practised hand felt above and to the left of the door. He pressed, and a panel inside sprang silently open. Then, carefully, he put his upper body inside the wardrobe and raised his candle. An exclamation escaped him. Quickly he took a small, clean bottle from his pocket, took down another from the concealed cupboard and tipped some of its contents into his own. Then he carefully returned the bottle to its shelf and shut the panel with a click.

In the nick of time. He heard a sound from the landing, and in an instant he was in the chair by the bed, his head bent in reverent pose. When Lady Hudson first tried the handle and then came through the door he held the pose for a second, then rose to his feet and stood by the chair.

'I thought I should keep watch, Your Ladyship,' he said, 'Sir Richard having been very good to me, God rest his soul.'

Lady Hudson, in her night robe, looked in the flickering light to be drawn and haggard – as why would she not be, having just lost her husband? She nodded distantly.

'That was very thoughtful, Joseph. Though a touch superstitious, perhaps. Almost Romish. Now I wish to be alone for a last time with my husband.'

Joseph inclined his head and left the death chamber, this time without any reluctance.

*

A Family in Mourning

It was in fact two days before Dr Packenham had an interview with Lady Hudson, though he sent his servant with respectful enquiries the day after Sir Richard's death. Pennywear, the butler, remarked that he would have expected a personal visit, as a matter of form. On the second day he wrote a note requesting a meeting if Lady Hudson's health and spirits should be equal to one, and suggesting that Sir Andrew and Miss Jane might also be present, as the melancholy details of the cause of their father's death must also have a mournful interest for them.

Lady Hudson was a mite perplexed by this. It became clearer to her when Dr Packenham paid his appointed visit. Shown into the small drawing room, he greeted them all gravely. He paid particular attention to the new baronet, commiserating with him on his loss and regretting the sombre responsibilities the death placed on him (ignoring the fact that as Andrew was a minor there were none). Asked to sit down he took a chair some way from the family, perched on the edge of his seat, and launched into a description of the causes of Sir Richard's death that would have done credit to a medical man in a novel.

'. . . A grave condition in itself, aggravated, I fear, by neglect . . . If Sir Richard had continued when in health taking the mixture I dispensed for him, some amelioration might have been expected . . . The fact is that with a strict regimen your father might have lived for years, but as you all know Sir Richard was the last person in the world to take good care of himself . . . I fear that the weakened condition of his heart, coming on top of the already serious attack of his usual complaint . . .'

In Lady Hudson the thought 'He sounds like a novel' soon developed into 'he is acting', especially when she realized he was really saying almost nothing of moment about the causes of Sir Richard's death. He's not committing himself, she thought, in case something comes out later on. When he had left, full of flowery commiserations to the last, but without responding to any of the surreptitious glances and silent enquiries she had sent in his direction, her thoughts developed into something still more galling and frightening.

He is putting a distance between himself and me, she thought.

*

It was on the day before the funeral that Joseph fired the first tentative shots in his campaign. His duties were now once more merely those of a footman, and when he and a maid had brought in Lady Hudson's afternoon tea he waited until the silver and china were satisfactorily set out, gestured to the maid Bessie to depart, and then cleared his throat.

'I wonder if I might have a word, Your Ladyship?'

Lady Hudson swallowed, but when she looked up it was with a bland and apparently friendly expression.

'Of course, Joseph.'

Joseph's own expression was to a degree respectful. His voice, too, was at its most formal, modelled as it was on Pennywear's.

'It occurred to me, Your Ladyship, that since Sir Richard was so sadly isolated by his illness those last few weeks, I might have been privy to his wishes and intentions now and then – may have known of intentions that he may not have found the opportunity to pass on to Your Ladyship.'

It was a piece of pure impertinence – a challenge thrown down. Inwardly boiling at the assumption of a greater intimacy with her dead husband than her own – justified though it was – Lady Hudson merely inclined her head.

'That may well be. We talked, when we could talk, mainly of my husband's sad state of health.'

'Exactly, Your Ladyship.' Joseph's speech now came down a step or two from its previous exaltation, being less well prepared. 'For example, the tutor, Mr Worsley. Sir Richard intended him to have the living of Little Burdock, but only on condition he got himself a wife. Said the parish had gone downhill since old Mrs Harmsworth died. Very insistent he was, Your Ladyship, that the person in that position needed to be a married man.'

'Yes, indeed, how wise of Sir Richard,' said his relict, but in a neutral tone.

'Then there was Sir Andrew as he now is. Sir Richard was of the opinion that, seeing as how he's rather young for his age, sending him to Cambridge wouldn't be the thing, 'specially with him not being used to the company of men of his own age. He thought he might go off the rails and get into a fast set. He was thinking of delaying him going to university, or maybe sending him to one of those new colleges in the north – Durham, maybe. He said it would keep him in touch with his roots, the source of his wealth.'

By now Lady Hudson was boiling with rage. To be in a situation which had the appearance of discussing her family with a footman! But she was too unsure of her position in relation to him to put him down: with an effort she managed to maintain her bland tone.

'How extraordinary! Do they have some kind of a college at Durham? My family has always gone to Cambridge.'

'Those were Sir Richard's wishes.'

There was silence from the chair by the fire. Joseph was unperturbed.

'And on the matter of Miss Jane. Thought Miss Jane needed to be married young, Sir Richard did – too headstrong for her own good, and needing a firm hand. As far as I can remember his very words were that she had a wilful intelligence that needed to be curbed. He thought the duties of a wife and mother would bring her to heel.'

Now Joseph had gone well beyond the decent. To discuss that matter with a footman would have amounted to some kind of admission. Lady Hudson felt she would have been justified in dismissing him, whatever his services to her late husband. She did not do so. She left a silence, as before, and then said: 'Thank you, Joseph. I will think over what you've said.'

Joseph bowed at his dismissal.

'Thank you, Your Ladyship. Only trying to be of assistance . . . Will Dr Packenham be coming after dinner, Your Ladyship?'

'I don't believe so. He has not said that he will.'

'Ah. I thought he might be assisting in arrangements for the funeral, Your Ladyship.'

When the door was shut Lady Hudson had to restrain herself from screaming with rage and frustration. To have any kind of discussion of family affairs with a servant – and a discussion initiated by him! – was bad enough. To have her children discussed with her, her daughter described as headstrong, her son, by implication, as weak-willed! And all under the guise of respect for her dead husband's wishes! The man was insufferable! And to question her about her visitors. Question her about Dr Packenham . . .

It was intolerable. He should be dismissed. But she knew in her heart that he would not be, that she could not bring herself to do it for fear of certain consequences. Because whatever she might later write to her mother, Lady Hudson was very uncertain where she stood with Joseph.

'More should not – cannot – be said on the subject which I opened up to you on the dreadful day of Sir Richard's death,' murmured William Worsley.

'Of course not,' agreed Frances Weyland. 'William.'

They were walking some way behind their charges in the grounds of Elmstead Court, all in deep mourning. The charges had been given strict instructions about their conduct which for once even the younger girls had obeyed. They doubtless felt, like the rest of Elmstead's inhabitants, that with Sir Richard's death they were entering an unknown country, whose contours and geographical features had yet to be mapped.

'Precipitate action, any action which might seem to indicate a lack of respect for the dead, is to be deplored.'

'Naturally,' said Miss Weyland, thinking what an absolutely typical clergyman Mr Worsley would make.

'I recur to the subject only to set your mind at rest that it is not forgotten, should we not have the chance to talk of it in the next weeks or months.'

'I thank you for your consideration, William.'

His words ought to have reassured her, but they did not. The next weeks or months! How could it come about that they would not have a chance to talk it over in the next *months*? Ludicrous. He was waiting to see how the land lay in the new dispensation, that was what Mr Worsley was doing.

Miss Weyland felt that her bird in the hand was in danger of flying off to become a second one in the bush.

*

MISS JANE HUDSON TO AN UNIDENTIFIED
CORRESPONDENT

Mr dear W.,

I have had a shock since dispatching my last. I can only pray
I am mistaken.

Two days after the funeral it was decided we would go into
the village. It had to be done sometime, and we had to nerve
ourselves to receive the condolences – sincere or otherwise –
of the village people. When I say 'we' I mean Miss Weyland,
my sisters, and myself, but when he heard of our intention
Andrew determined to accompany us. Our destination was
Mr Weston's shop, which sells Manchester goods, and Mrs
Turner's provisions shop, which also accepts letters for
dispatch. I had with me my last to you.

We made an odd enough looking group, I dare say: all in
black, and conversing, if at all, in the most clipped and muted
tones of voice. I wonder where our present-day notions of
mourning decorum come from, and when they started. Did
the family of a country gentleman a hundred years ago make
such a po-faced spectacle of themselves, I wonder? I
remember your remarks about how much freer and more
natural the behaviour of older people is, compared to the
dreadfully inhibited conduct of the young today. I asked
Andrew about funerals and mourning, talking low and serious
as we made a pair behind the other three, and he said he
would find out. He agreed that we all made a ridiculous
spectacle.

'And for such a man!' he added bitterly.

Several of the villagers came up to express their condolences,
usually to Andrew. Sensible people! He will one day be their
Squire and Master. I begin to understand and laud self-
interest, you note. What other doctrine or rule can the poor
and helpless live their lives by? Andrew received their
expressions of sorrow gravely, fittingly: he will be a good
diplomatist. Mr Weston tried to combine condolences to
Andrew and us all with satisfying our needs in the cotton and
wool lines, and made a fearful hash of the combination. Miss

Weyland got confused, my sisters were in danger of giggling, so we made a couple of purchases and retreated from the shop.

Our visits to Mrs Turner's are always to dispatch letters, of course, though as children we sometimes purchased sweetmeats there. I must say that I have never liked the woman. There is a sort of wheedling familiarity about her that I find offensive, and so it could not but be that I should find her expressions of sympathy distasteful. Feeling the same, and having no letter to post, Andrew said he would wait outside. It occurs to me that Andrew, unlike most boys of his age, has *no friend*, never having been sent away to school. It is a great deprivation for one who aims to make his way in the larger world. And he is, I believe, for all his shyness, a very lovable person.

The shop, as always, was dark and overcrowded, and we had no sooner entered than Mrs Turner began her inevitable rigmarole about our loss, the village's loss, such a fine man, a man everyone looked up to, and so on, and so on. We murmured agreement and tried to transact our business and as my eyes became accustomed to the gloom I realized that for once Mrs Turner was not alone behind her counter: there was a large, heavy woman, well wrapped up in black down at the far end, with sharp black eyes under low lids, and a secretive, threatening air. At length she flicked her tongue around her lips and came towards us.

'Would you permit a stranger to add 'er condolences, young ladies? I've known loss, I 'ave, when my dear 'usband was took, so I know 'ow it feels.'

'Oh, this is Mrs . . . Hill,' said Mrs Turner hurriedly. 'She's helping me out here for a bit.'

We acknowledged Mrs Hill's presence, thanked her for her sympathy, insincere as I felt it to be, and handed over our pennies and our letters. Mrs Turner was still in full flood of condolence as we retreated from the shop and rejoined Andrew' in the sunlight.

'What an unpleasant woman!' I said.

'Jane!' said Miss Weyland reprovingly. We were out of earshot, so she must have felt any expression of opinion at this

time to be a breach of decorum. Andrew and I resumed our positions at the rear of the funeral column and once more conversed in low voices.

'Who? Mrs Turner?' he asked.

'No, though she is. Another woman. Helping Mrs Turner out, apparently. Why should she need help all of a sudden? She has no great number of customers.'

'Why was this woman objectionable?'

'Oh, she was horrible – her manner, her *self* . . . She reminded me of someone . . . the face . . . the voice . . . the accent. I can't think who it is . . . Oh!'

'What?'

'I've realized who it is. She reminds me of Joseph.'

I saw Andrew's face darken.

In the little shop the two women looked ahead of them as the door shut and the little party went off down the street. Then they looked at each other.

'Shall I put the kettle on?' said Mrs Kate Morrissey.

CHAPTER THIRTEEN

Setbacks and Steps Forward

It was not easy for Joseph to get a day off. In the old days, of course, it would have been child's play: Sir Richard, if he was in health, would simply have granted it to him and Joseph himself would have told Pennywear, who would have gritted his teeth and nodded sourly. It would have been possible, in the new dispensation of things at Elmstead Court, for Joseph to have used his growing but nebulous power over Lady Hudson to procure a similar permission, but for various reasons he did not want her to know that he was going outside the immediate vicinity of Elmstead Court. He therefore, like a cat with a bird in view, bided his time, knowing that at some stage there would be household business coming up at Marwick, Matham, or Denge, the three country towns closest to Elmstead, any one of which would have suited his purposes.

Nearly three weeks after Elmstead Court went into mourning Lady Hudson expressed a wish for turbot, her favourite fish. She was especially fond of it braised with scallops, mushrooms, and artichokes. Turbot would certainly not be readily available in Elmstead, and Joseph volunteered to ride over to Matham.

'I'd do anything for her ladyship,' he said.

'Naturally if her ladyship expresses a wish we all do our utmost to see it fulfilled,' said Pennywear austerely. 'Especially at the present time.'

Sentimental expressions of devotion were not in Pennywear's

line, and he certainly didn't trust any that came from Joseph. If
there was ever a man on the make, Pennywear felt, that man
was Joseph. However, he gave permission for him to go to
Matham, and Joseph, chafing at the need to have permission
and vowing to himself that the situation would soon change,
expressed his gratitude.

Once out of sight of the house Joseph dug his heels into Barker,
the hack horse he was riding, and gained Elmstead village in a
matter of minutes. He tied Barker to the post in the square and
went to Mrs Turner's for a hurried consultation with his mother.
They retreated into the back of the shop and conversed in low
voices, which Mrs Turner regarded as unfriendly. She had only
agreed to take in Mrs Morrissey in the expectation of being part
of whatever was going on.

'He's a wonderful boy,' was all Mrs Morrissey said when her
son had hastened off. 'He'll go far.'

Mrs Turner shot her a sour look.

Barker was a horse that it was impossible to incite to speed
for any length of time. Thus it was almost midday by the time
Joseph arrived in Matham. Once he had left Barker in temporary
stabling he walked down the High Street enjoying the compara-
tive bustle of the small market town, and going over in his mind
his plan of campaign for the hoped-for interview that was to
follow. The doctor's establishment he made for was one unknown
to the Hudson family and household, the man himself never
having been called in for a second opinion by Dr Packenham.
He was, however, a young man with an excellent reputation,
and he and his assistant did their own dispensing. When he was
shown into the consulting room Joseph blenched a little at the
authority stamped on Dr McClelland's face: it was one of those
chiselled Scottish faces which seemed to have angles where more
southern faces had curves. His eyes were blue and sharp and he
had a peppery little moustache. By now Joseph was in the room
and being looked at enquiringly, and he had no option but to
plunge into the pottage of mendacity he had prepared on his
ride. The voice he chose as most appropriate to his assumed
role was something between his footman's tones and his natural
speaking voice.

'Sorry I'm sure to trouble you, Doctor, but it's about a very delicate matter, something my master is sadly troubled by—'

'Your master?'

'A reverend gentleman, elderly like, and retired from the Church. You won't have heard of him. The Reverend Walter Smith, from over Elmstead way.'

'And you are?'

'Naylor, Edward Naylor.'

'Very well. And so to this delicate matter.'

Joseph found his manner very disconcerting.

'It's . . . it's a question of medicine, Doctor. Mr Smith has had prescribed for him for some time now a sort of tonic for the 'eart — by Dr Packenham—'

Joseph shot a look at Dr McClelland, who sat in the chair behind his desk, totally impassive.

'—and this last time the tonic came — made up, of course, from Dr Packenham's — my master said as how it tasted different and had a very nasty effect on him, not wanting to go into details. Now, he's sure that what it must be is that Dr Packenham's made a mistake in the dispensing of it, but it worries my master — him being a gentleman of conscience, no one more so, and he wonders if he's justified in saying naught about it, seeing as how the doctor may have made other mistakes with other medicines, or may be like to make them in the future.'

Joseph paused to draw breath, hoping for an encouraging word or two from the man before him, but getting none. Feeling desperately the need to add verisimilitude to his story he took from his pocket the small bottle.

'So he thought, if you could examine this stuff — analyse was his word I believe — and tell him what's in it, it would set his mind at rest if the stuff is harmless and quite safe to take for a gentleman with a weak 'eart. And if, on the other hand, there's been a bad mistake, then Mr Smith will have to meditate his course of action, to use his own words, though as Dr Packenham is a personal friend, and busy in charitable concerns in the neighbourhood, it's unlikely as how he'd do more than have a quiet word — sort of show him as how he ought to take more care . . .'

Joseph wound down to a halt. There was silence in the room, and Joseph had never been more conscious of the ticking of a clock. Then Dr McClelland stirred in his chair.

'Well, man, I've heard you out. I can only say this: I don't know what your real name is, nor what your real business is, but to my eye you do not have the look of an honest man. I smell cock, and I smell bull. The door is there. Good day to you.'

If Joseph had had a tail, and it would have been a perfectly appropriate appendage, it would assuredly have been between his legs as he slunk from the house.

On the day that Joseph made his expedition to Matham Mr Worsley decided he had banking business in Marwick which had been delayed by the death and the funeral, but which now could be put off no longer. As he was pointing out to his pupil some relevant material in the library on the subject of the Restoration and General Monk's role in it he was surprised by a request from Andrew to accompany him. He had sundry small purchases to make, he said, and he felt dull and frowsty after the mental turmoil of the last two weeks. Mr Worsley promised to put his request to Lady Hudson, and he found her surprisingly sympathetic.

'The boy has had a great deal of strain and . . . distress these last few weeks,' she said. 'As we all have.'

'Yes, indeed,' murmured Mr Worsley.

'Of course the boy shall go with you if he wants to.' When Mr Worsley showed signs of getting up to go, Lady Hudson cut in quickly with: 'The death of Sir Richard, as well as being a grievous loss in itself—'

'Grievous indeed.'

'—leaves those of us who are left behind with added burdens.'

'Your Ladyship must surely find them heavy. And coming, in the nature of things, at such a time of sorrow . . .'

Lady Hudson nodded.

'But I was not thinking only of myself. Though to have decisions to make and *no one* to discuss them with is hard indeed.

But there are increased burdens for others too. You yourself, Mr Worsley, have long held a position of trust and responsibility in relation to Andrew. The gravity of your responsibilities must increase, now that you stand, in a sense, in the position of father to the boy – the nearest thing to a father he now has.'

'I shall of course endeavour always to be worthy of Your Ladyship's trust.'

It may be that Mr Worsley's face had dropped at the mention of his increased responsibilities: he would not commit the vulgarity (Mr Worsley never did commit vulgarities) of asking how much substitute parenthood paid, and neither could he at this stage mention his urgent desire to slip the yoke of Elmstead Court and flit to fresh (and rich) pasturage. Nevertheless something got through to Lady Hudson that spoke of concern, even consternation.

'I'm sure you will. And I know that Sir Richard was intending to reward your great devotion to the family, and your *excellent* endeavours with Andrew, in an appropriate way. You had, I believe, discussed this?'

'We had touched on the matter, yes,' said William Worsley, keeping the surprise out of his voice, but feeling his heart leap. 'We talked the matter over in London.'

'So I gathered . . . from Sir Richard. The living of Little Burdock I believe it was that was discussed?'

'Your Ladyship is too kind to bring the matter up, especially at such a time. Yes, it was Little Burdock that was mentioned. Sir Richard felt—'

'Sir Richard felt that the parish, little by little, was going to rot – not to put too fine a point on it. I must say that in my own work – my charitable work – in the area I have seen many distressing things that lead me to agree with him. Mr Harmsworth is an excellent man – a gentleman, and conscientious in his time. But he is, as the funeral so painfully showed, an *old* man, and since Mrs Harmsworth died . . .'

'Yes, that was Sir Richard's feeling, and my own too. My impression is that since she died he has been unable to take over and do himself things – pastoral things – that Mrs Harmsworth performed well and unobtrusively.' Mr Worsley pulled himself up: *that* argument for replacing Mr Harmsworth should not be over-stressed. 'If he had been a bachelor throughout his life, perhaps—'

'Yes?'

'—perhaps things would have been different. A Roman Catholic priest, for instance, need not be hampered by his single state.'

'My family has always prided itself on its *Protestant* principles,' said Lady Hudson coldly. This was no less than the truth. The Walton-Smiths had clung to their Protestant principles with a tenacity only equalled by that with which they clung to the lands and treasures of a Lincolnshire abbey, despoiled by them in 1539.

'Oh, of course, of course,' said Mr Worsley, feeling himself floundering, and wishing he had never fallen into the comparison. 'A Roman Catholic priest stands in a *very* different relationship with his flock – more that of a *master* to children – very regrettable and antique, and quite unsuitable in England in the nineteenth century. Whereas a Protestant clergyman . . .'

'Yes?'

'Well, a Protestant clergyman adds the pastoral to the spiritual, and he must lead by example: the example of the good life, joyfully followed.'

Mr Worsley felt he was spouting nonsense, but he did so with all the conviction he could muster.

'I am glad that we agree on that,' said Lady Hudson, with apparent satisfaction. 'It was this example that Sir Richard felt Mr Harmsworth was failing to give, as a widower. And things in the parish were falling through his fingers – still are, I feel sure.' She was talking more confidently now, as if this were a matter which she and her husband had frequently discussed, though they never had. 'It was for this reason that Sir Richard felt it necessary to insist that the new incumbent should be a married man.'

Mr Worsley kept his face, this time, impassive.

'We did indeed discuss—'

Lady Hudson held up her hand.

'This is not a matter we should go into now. Early days, indeed, with Sir Richard hardly cold in his grave. And your work with Andrew is still far from finished.'

'It was thought, Lady Hudson, that my tutorship of Sir Andrew might be continued at Little Burdock – that he might come and live in the Rectory, and I might combine the two avocations.'

Lady Hudson nodded, pensively.

'Ah – so that had been thought of. Certainly the needs of that parish are pressing. On the other hand it would be a grievous loss, *now*, to have the one man of the family removed from Elmstead Court. I must steel myself, perhaps, to make that sacrifice for the general good.' She looked, in fact, as if she might be able to bear having Andrew's critical eye removed from her. 'We will discuss this further, Mr Worsley.'

'You are too kind, Lady Hudson. Perhaps I should just add that on the . . . the matrimonial subject, things are – well, to go no further: things are in train.'

Lady Hudson smiled and nodded her dismissal. Mr Worsley dipped his head and withdrew. With his mouth he was smiling, but in his heart he was saying 'Damn!'

The ride from Elmstead Court to Marwick was a difficult one, consisting mainly of narrow lanes and footpaths that could only be travelled in single file. Conversation between William Worsley and Andrew was therefore impossible, and in fact silence suited both men. Andrew could meditate the purpose of his errand and the tactics he should employ, while Mr Worsley was entertaining a new idea that had come to him since his conversation that morning with Lady Hudson.

When they arrived in Marwick and had stabled their horses the two separated, after briefly consulting about the time for their journey home.

'I may drop in on Mr Thurston, the rural dean,' said Mr Worsley casually. 'An old friend.'

Andrew temporized by going to a saddler's just off the High

Street and buying himself a new whip and riding gloves. He took his time in pricing and comparing, to ensure that Mr Worsley was well about his business, then he made his way to Warlock and Winterburn, the firm of solicitors which had dealt with Hudson family business since Sir Richard's father, feeling suddenly dynastic after spending his life in the cut-throat world of mills and markets, had purchased Elmstead Court for his son in 1825, the year of Andrew's birth, from an elderly roué and gambler who had dissipated his inheritance across Europe in the years since Waterloo. In the solicitors' main office a middle-aged clerk first looked at Andrew quizzically. Then, seeing that, in spite of the schoolboyish appearance, he was undoubtedly dressed as a gentleman as well as having the air of one, the clerk came over and respectfully enquired his business.

'Is it possible to see Mr Winterburn? It is on Hudson family business. I am Sir Andrew Hudson.'

It was a measure of Andrew's increased confidence since the death of his father, as well, perhaps, of the effect a title has on the middle ranks of society, that the clerk immediately became immensely respectful, ushering him to a comfortable chair and bustling off to consult with Mr Winterburn. It was hardly more than a minute before the solicitor, elderly but spry, came out from his own office, hand outstretched.

'Sir Andrew! My deepest condolences, sir. My deepest sympathy. A melancholy and sadly premature end to a distinguished life. But it is a great pleasure to make your acquaintance. Come through, sir. We have not had the pleasure before, I think? No, I thought not. You were still in the schoolroom last time I dined at Elmstead. Changes, changes. Well, all the more reason to talk things over now. Your mother is bearing up well, is she?'

He ushered Andrew ahead of him into his office, while Andrew himself responded with murmured platitudes. Once inside he noticed that the clerk was gestured to fetch a decanter and glasses which stood on the massive sideboard. As he was conducted to a comfortable leather chair in front of the desk a glass of port was respectfully placed in front of him. A sense of well-being, a sense that this was the life, flowed through Andrew.

'Apart from being a pleasure, Sir Andrew,' said Mr Winterburn, seating himself behind his desk and taking up his own glass, 'this is a most valuable opportunity.' He sipped from the cut glass with legal caution. 'It is time – as no doubt you would agree – to acquaint you with your position and prospects, if your late father did not do so before his untimely death.'

Andrew, sipping and then nodding acquiescence, thought that he had seldom been so lucky: the apple had fallen into his lap without his even having to shake the branch. His fatherless state was proving to be everything he had hoped. He sat back in his chair with a pretence of relaxation while Mr Winterburn began his exposition of his position and prospects.

Mr Worsley transacted his business at the bank quite quickly. It was to arrange for the transfer of a small sum of money – small sums were all that William Worsley ever had to do with – to the woman who looked after his mother. That lady had had the misfortune to lose her wits very early in life, though her situation was alleviated by a quarterly gift from a charitable society that aided distressed gentlefolk. Mr Worsley's father had died when he was ten. Much of the calculation which ruled Mr Worsley's life sprang from the fact that his circumstances called for it.

When he came out of the bank Mr Worsley turned to the right and made his way to a substantial house built in the reign of Queen Anne, a house which he had often remarked on but had never been into. At the door he enquired for Mr Thurston, and as he waited in the hall he noted the many evidences of comfort and prosperity.

His reception, when the maid showed him into the rural dean's study, was both courteous and friendly. Mr Thurston may have been curious as to what he owed this honour, but he was careful to hide the emotion.

'We have met, have we not?' he asked his young visitor. 'Will it have been at Elmstead Court? Yes, of course it was at Elmstead. And you were perhaps at lunch after the service? Yes, indeed. The death of Sir Richard – so young, so comparatively young – saddened me immensely. Lady Hudson is bearing up, I trust?'

'As well as can be expected. Though Sir Richard had been ill for some time she had hardly contemplated that the illness might be mortal, or at least that the end would be so sudden. It is as a consequence of speaking with Lady Hudson that I am venturing to trespass on your time, Mr Thurston.'

'Yes?'

Mr Worsley sat forward in his chair, an earnest expression on his face.

'As you will know, Mr Harmsworth at Little Burdock has been anxious for some time to give up the cares of the parish.'

'Ah! He has not confided in me, but I am not surprised.'

'Sir Richard was anxious before he died to have the parish in the hands of a younger man.'

'Wise man. A very sensible decision. He was in many ways an excellent judge of things.'

'He had expressed his intention of bestowing the living on me.' Mr Worsley's face now assumed an expression of modest satisfaction. 'Lady Hudson has just intimated to me that she wishes to abide by that decision, either when Sir Andrew goes to university, or perhaps earlier, if suitable arrangements can be made.'

Mr Thurston rubbed his hands and beamed and made all the congratulatory noises that are usual when someone has come into good fortune.

'My dear sir, this is excellent news! For you, of course – it's a very good living – but also for the parish. Will you take a glass of wine with me?'

Mr Worsley could only be delighted by the reception of his news. Over the glass of wine he discussed with the rural dean the state of the parish of Little Burdock, then nudged the conversation gently in the direction of his own circumstances, the sad state of his mother's health, and his great good fortune in finding so congenial a position at Elmstead Court. From there it was but a natural step to enquiring after the dean's own family.

'Mrs Thurston is well, I trust?'

'Never better – blooming!'

'I had the good fortune to meet Mrs Thurston at Elmstead Court, but not the two Misses Thurston.'

'Ah, they are blooming too.' The good dean beamed again with paternal pride. 'But my elder daughter is married: to a gentleman in the woollen trade. We must not despise trade in these times, you know, and he is in a very good way. But his trade is in Glasgow, and we miss our girl sadly.'

'I'm sure you must. I imagine you will hope to keep your other daughter closer to you here in Hampshire.'

'We do indeed. You saw the announcement?'

'Announcement?'

'In the *Hampshire and Berkshire Gazette*. Astonishing to find our little Julia engaged to be married! But he is an excellent man, and in orders – curate to Mr Liversedge at Great Moffat. We love him already like a son.'

Though Mr Worsley kept the conversation going for another quarter of an hour, the spice seemed to have gone out of his visit. He took his leave, leaving Mr Thurston rather puzzled as to why he had not enquired after his son. On the ride home he was preoccupied, and did not notice the air of quiet satisfaction which his pupil exuded.

CHAPTER FOURTEEN

Coming Out Into the Open

Mrs Turner was less than happy with her new lodger and helper. It was all very well to have someone to share the gossip and conjecture which had always been an essential part of her life in the village, and she was willing, too, to have a partner in those mildly nefarious activities which added a further spice to her existence – particularly if it was understood that they were both equally culpable, and if one was caught both were caught. But it began to dawn on her quite early that partners they certainly were not: that though Mrs Morrissey was avid to be given information, she was extremely cagey about giving it in return. Thus, though she had been in Elmstead two weeks and more, Mrs Turner was still little the wiser about her reasons for being there, beyond that they concerned Elmstead Court.

'There's things afoot at the 'Ouse,' her lodger would say, 'as you wouldn't believe, not in a thousand years.' Which, as Mrs Turner said resentfully to herself, didn't get you very far. Later modifications of this were hardly more substantial. 'There'll be a scandal at the big 'Ouse as'll rock the 'ole county,' Mrs Morrissey would say. 'Unless my Joe can keep the lid on it.'

Yes, but what would the scandal consist of, Mrs Turner asked, first of herself, later of the lady herself. Mrs Morrissey shook her head ominously, and pursed her lips.

'More than my life's worth to tell you,' she replied in doom-laden tones. 'But if my Joe doesn't get 'is way, then everyone'll know soon enough.'

In this last prophecy the lady was being disingenuous, for she both hoped and expected that the lid would be kept on the Hudson family scandal, to the advantage of herself and her son. As had happened in the case of the Duke. Though that gentleman's untimely death had robbed Mrs Morrissey of a milch cow, and the milk she had extracted had long since been consumed.

The frustration of Mrs Turner's natural curiosity became acute on the morning after Joseph's abortive visit to Matham. He was on House business in Elmstead, and he took time off to slip in and see his mother. They both retreated once again into the back room of the shop, which was just far enough away from the counter for them to converse unheard if they kept their voices down. This they did not entirely manage to do, and in the intervals of attending to the wants of her customers Mrs Turner heard words like 'blockhead' and 'booby' – words that seemed violently to escape Mrs Morrissey from a force of emotion she could not suppress. She also heard a bitter reproach: 'You could 'ave done for yourself – and if you 'ave, don't bring me into it.' These words alarmed Mrs Turner, for they suggested the thought that if Mrs Morrissey could be 'brought into it', then so might she herself. There was that letter of Miss Jane's, though admittedly she had only had sections of it read out to her. Nevertheless she had winked at its being opened.

She peered into the back room. Something small was being passed from son to mother, only to disappear into the capacious black draperies which were her everyday costume. Mrs Turner's uneasiness increased, and was not assuaged when Joseph marched out, face black as night, banged through the shop and slammed the street door shut, setting the bell a-jangle. She was, however, more than a little afraid of her house guest, and when Kate Morrissey came back into the shop and sat some way apart, her expression sulphurous, she said nothing. When, later in the day, her lodger emerged from this purdah and began asking questions, Mrs Turner responded forgivingly. She had always enjoyed giving information, and was at no loss for it when Mrs Morrissey turned the conversation to medical practitioners in the nearby towns.

'A *young* man is 'e?' Mrs Morrissey would respond, in an attempt at good fellowship. 'Oh, fairly young. I prefer an older man meself . . . Ah, 'e's an elderly gentleman, is 'e? That's what I like. Old school. They 'ave some respect for a body. Ah, one of the Denge doctors. Failing in 'is eyesight, is 'e? But 'e knows 'is business? What was 'is name again?'

Mrs Turner would very much like to have fathomed the motive behind her lodger's interest, but that lady played her cards very close to her bombazined bosom.

Miss Jane Hudson to an Unidentified Correspondent

A curious thing has happened – a small thing, but curious indeed. My mother has opened the subject of marriage, but that is not it: that I half expected, as you know from my last (of which more later). It was the manner of her bringing the matter up which so intrigued me.

She had asked me to take tea with her this afternoon, and I went expecting to have my sympathies solicited for her lonely state, the magnitude of her loss, and the weight of her responsibilities. Do I sound unsympathetic? I am not, and I have always had until now a certain respect for my mother. But I am finding I am having to cultivate a hard shell to present to the world, for it expects of me things that I am not willing to give.

We were alone, and Joseph and one of the maids officiated, bringing the sandwiches, cake, and tea, until eventually Joseph stood by Mama's chair and asked: 'Will that be all, Your Ladyship?'

'Yes, that will be all, Joseph,' said Mama. Then, before Joseph had left the room Mama said to me in a hurried, embarrassed way: 'What I wanted to discuss with you, Jane dear, was your marriage.'

That was the small but significant incident. Does this really sound natural to you? That the matter should be brought up thus, so brusquely? Surely in such a case a mother prepares the ground, cushions the shock of a difficult subject in advance? Yet my mother simply brandished the matter at me without preliminaries. More importantly, she brought it up while the footman was still in the room, even though he was on his way out of it. Why not wait a moment or two? Then again, the servant was Joseph. If it had been Pennywear I should perhaps have thought no more than that my mother had been clumsy, inept (*though she is seldom either of those things*). But Joseph!

For my mother has no love for Joseph, that you must already have guessed. To call her feelings jealousy would perhaps be to give a wrong impression, but I feel sure that she resented his place in my father's life, a place that grew in importance week by week, month by month, and which displaced her. That resentment she had, in my father's time, to *hide*. I feel sure that is one of the reasons why she . . . But I must take care. I have nothing more than suspicion to go on. At any rate, I am sure Mama feels nothing but repulsion and mistrust for Joseph, as all of us do, as all *must* do, except for my father. And what did *he* feel? Did he share the repulsion, but enjoy parading Joseph and his special position before the family and servants, enjoy the impotent feelings of disgust and anger that he aroused? Who can know? Who could fathom such a man?

I let some time elapse after Joseph had closed the door, then said: 'There is no question of my marrying, Mama.'

My mother certainly understood the significance of the pause, for she looked still more flustered when she replied.

'Well, of course, I was not necessarily suggesting that you entertained thoughts of Mr Page . . . Though your father—'

I cut in quickly.

'My father was on his deathbed, probably unclear in his mind, and in any case did not make his intentions clear. But all those considerations are irrelevant. Even if he had been sound in mind and body and had expressed himself clearly, I would not then and I will not now marry Mr James Page.'

My mother, with that uncertainty which is uncharacteristic of her, but which is growing, retreated hurriedly.

'Well, of course, as I said there is no question of my insisting . . . if you feel that way about him . . . though he is personable enough . . . But I was speaking generally, Jane dear.'

'So was I, Mama. When I said that there was no question of my marrying I meant precisely that: I do not intend ever to marry.'

This declaration rallied my mother, as being patently absurd. She at last resumed her usual tones.

'What nonsense, Jane! I would have thought that you, of all people, would be above such missish silliness!'

'This is not a piece of silliness, Mama, and not some sudden whim which I shall forget about the moment a presentable young man turns up. I have thought long and seriously on the subject. So have many other people – Mr Owen and Mr Maurice and many more. It is time for a woman to take up the cause of her own sex. It is time for women to be properly educated, so that they may take their place in the conduct of the nation's affairs. We have a queen now, Mama, instead of mad or doddering old kings. It is time for women to free themselves from men's yoke. I could only help in that great struggle as an unmarried woman.'

My mother was dumbfounded, as I intended she should be.

'Well! I have never in my life heard such wicked nonsense! Where do you get such crazed notions from?'

'I thought them myself, Mama. They are in the air.'

'They are certainly not in the air I breathe! And how, pray, do you propose to support yourself while you conduct this irreligious crusade?'

'I shall eventually be able to support myself by teaching and writing. Until then Andrew will help me.'

'Then you will have to wait until he reaches his majority, for I will have nothing to do with it.'

'I can wait. I will try to educate myself – take that as far as it will go, before seeking a wider education for myself.'

My mother took refuge in false comfort.

'These are foolish notions that will pass.'

'They will not pass, Mama. I will never marry. Were you and Papa so happy in the married state that you would regard it as the only admissible goal in a woman's life?'

Mama puffed up with outrage, but there was fear there too.

'Jane! That is a disgraceful suggestion! Your father and I were devoted to each other.'

'At first, no doubt. I've heard you tell how fiery and determined he was, how he overcame all your family's opposition. I can understand how exciting it must have been to see grandmama worsted. But lately, Mama? Lately?'

'To the end!' she rapped out.

'I don't think so. I think you found that fire and determination had a reverse side to them.' I got up. 'I'll go now, Mama. I'm sorry to have upset you. Do think about what I have said. It will be impossible to change my mind.'

So the subject has been broached! I am glad of it, though I am aware that I must have sounded an intolerable little prig. Of course I knew Mama would never understand, let alone sympathize. She comes, as I've said before, from a generation of women who were nourished on romantic notions and who as a consequence centred their lives on men. But now at least she knows my views and my intentions. She will work against them, but what can she do? At dinner she said, while Joseph was in the room: 'Jane has got some fantastical idea of never marrying, Andrew. Have you ever heard of anything so silly? It must be some modern notion going around, one that flies straight in the face of the Bible. Of course she will marry when the time comes.'

'And how will you force me, Mama?' I said, keeping my tone light. 'The time is past when the Lucy Ashtons of this world could be forced to the altar.'

'That was her brother,' said Andrew. 'I'll never force you to the altar, Janey.'

Dear Andrew.

And now one final question. Did my letters concerning my father's death give signs of having been opened? I ask hardly expecting an answer, for, with your poor eyesight, I cannot hope that you will have noticed, especially as when you received them you had not been alerted to the new woman in Mrs Turner's shop. The more I think about her the more I connect her with Joseph. Is that because so much that is happening at Elmstead seems to lead back to Joseph? I don't think so. Her face was at first much concealed by shawls and scarves, but when she came up to offer 'condolences' (impertinencies) I could see it clearly. It was Joseph's!

I shall never dispatch letters from there again. This I am entrusting to one of the maids, who is tomorrow visiting her father in Matham. She visits him once a fortnight, so be assured: if letters from me are less frequent in the future, they will as a consequence be even longer!

Your friend

Jane Hudson

Mrs Kate Morrissey started early the next morning on her journey to Denge, wrapped up against the first nip of autumn in a voluminous bundle of capes and coats that made her look from a distance like a walking Christmas pudding. Several carts and the odd coach passed her on the road, but only one of them stopped and offered her a ride. This was a farmer, who saved her two miles of her walk. So profuse was she in her gratitude, and so persistent in her enquiries about himself and his family, that the farmer was relieved when the time came to let her down. Mrs Morrissey would not have been surprised at this reaction, or displeased. Creating feelings of unease or disgust in those who could not escape her was one of her pleasures in life. Nevertheless she was aware that she must make a very different impression when she reached her goal.

Denge was the most depressing of the towns within easy reach of Elmstead. The farming was poor, the biggest landowner an absentee with a screw for an agent. Its main street was a mean collection of shops, offices, and residences, none of them aspiring to anything beyond the utilitarian. Mrs Morrissey thought the place might suit her purposes very well. The medical men serving this population would hardly be of the first rank. She observed the poor people scurrying or hobbling about their business, thought herself into their lives and ways, though with a tinge of contempt for them in her enterprising brain. Then she stopped one of them and asked the way to Dr Dawkins's house.

The doctor lived in a heavy, shady old house five minutes' walk from the main street. Mrs Morrissey represented herself to the housemaid as a stranger in Denge, in great need of a talk with a medical man. Within minutes she was being ushered in to the doctor's presence. Already well muffled, she had pulled a scarf over the lower part of her face, aware that her appearance did not prepossess people in her favour.

'This is kind,' she murmured, 'and much appreciated. My daughter said as you was the kindest gentleman to the poor and needy, and she spoke nothing less than the truth.'

Dr Dawkins had, indeed, something of the look of Mr Pickwick, and exuded an aura of general and perhaps unthinking benevolence. A close observer (and Mrs Morrissey was one) might have guessed that he was not the sharpest of practitioners, or the one most abreast of modern theories and treatments. The spectacles perched on his nose were very thick, but even with them he seemed to see with difficulty.

'Well, well, my good woman, I do my best. We none of us can do more. Your daughter, you say—?'

'Mrs Cranbrook. You won't 'ave 'eard of 'er – a very 'ealthy woman, God be thanked. But she knows all about your goodness to those whose need is greatest.'

'And your own problem, Mrs—?'

'Mrs Marryatt. Widowed these many years, God be—' she had very nearly said 'God be praised', an accurate reflection of her thoughts on the matter, but she hurriedly amended it – 'God's will be done. Well, Doctor, to come to the point, my problem's not so much a medical one, as what you might call a personal one. Not that I don't 'ave my trials to bear, and there's the rub, as you might say. Because Dr Willett's been very good to me, that I'd tell anybody. I come from Wiltshire – Trowbridge way – and I 'ave problems with me legs – a sort of gout, Dr Willett says – and with me 'eart too. So I'm not strong, though God be praised it could be worse, and there's many as suffers

more, that I'm well aware. But Dr Willett's been giving me –
no charge 'e makes – a medicine that's done me ever so much
good up to now. And then, just before I come away to visit me
daughter, 'e gives me a new bottle, because run out I was about
to, and needed more to bring with me, and I took some three
days ago, feeling just a bit poorly. And, Doctor, the effects was
'orrible!'

'What sort of effects?'

'Throwing up and the rest, details not being needed, as I'm
sure you understand, and feeling all over faint, and like to die –
'ardly knowing what was going on around me.'

'Could you have eaten something that disagreed with you?'

He peered at her, as if to detect signs of food poisoning, but
he could see little beyond a black blur of scarves and capes.

'Well, that's the thing, Doctor,' said Mrs Morrissey, giving
the appearance of very much wanting him to be right. 'Because
fish we had eaten, on the Friday, and though I 'ad smelt it and
thought it fresh as morning dew, and me daughter said the same,
still, I'm getting to be an old woman, and who's to say we might
not 'ave been mistook and it was a bit orf?'

'It would have had to be very off to have such an effect.'

'That's what I thought, Doctor. And me daughter ate 'er
share, an' she's been right as rain. Now, our Dr Willett is the
kindest gentleman to us poor, but 'e's 'igh with it, and not one
to cross, and I dursent go back to 'im and say, "There's summat
wrong with that medicine you gave me, Doctor, and could I 'ave
another bottle made up in the old way?" for fear 'e'd take offence,
like I was accusing 'im of making an awful mistake.'

'Of course, of course,' Dr Dawkins beamed. 'And you'd like
me to analyse the medicine – ah, you have some there, do you?
– and see if there's anything wrong with it, would you? Perfectly
simple . . . Hmm, that's a slightly odd smell. Now, you'll be
staying at your daughter's for a bit, will you? Shall we say the
day after tomorrow? Come and see me then and I'll tell you if
it's safe to take the rest of the bottle. If not, I'll make you up
something myself. No, no – don't thank me. Just as well to be
sure, isn't it? Better safe than sorry, that's my motto.'

But old Mrs Morrissey, hobbling out with much greater

difficulty than she in fact had with walking, really did feel something that was as close as she could come to gratitude. It had all been so much easier than she had expected.

MISS FRANCES WEYLAND TO MISS LYDIA PORSON

My dearest Lydia,

Thanks, *many* thanks, for your interesting if all too brief letter, which I would have replied to ere now had it not been for the dreadful events – quite unforeseen in my last – which have overtaken us all here at Elmstead Court. You will have seen the notice of Sir Richard's death in *The Times*, and I will add only that his family and friends, and indeed his dependants such as myself, are *prostrated* with grief, though Lady Hudson has been strengthened and supported by the love of her children, and begins to take up the reins Sir Richard can no longer wield.

I write now, dearest Lydia, to tell you my news. I am an engaged woman! Yesterday afternoon Mr Worsley, the new Sir Andrew's tutor, found me in the rose garden, and I could tell by the strong emotion evident in his face, and in his voice and bearing, that he intended something – and indeed he had skirted around the subject more than once in recent weeks, as if trying to pluck up the courage, but the *grief* of this stricken household had hitherto prevented him from speaking. But yesterday, looking me passionately in the eyes, he declared that he has admired me from the moment I came to Elmstead, that for months he has loved me, and that only thoughts of his poverty have prevented him from speaking, but that now, with the promise of a living in the vicinity, he had determined to speak his love and ask me to make him the happiest of men. I gazed at him, enthralled by his passion, and for the first time *told my love* and said *yes* to his urgent and ardent pleas.

So – I am an engaged woman, and the betrothal is not quite so imprudent a matter as I said in my earlier letter that any such engagement would be. Lady Hudson has given him a definite promise of a living some ten miles from Elmstead, and a good one too! But worldly matters are very far from my thoughts at this moment, for this is a *love match*, and will, I trust, finally give the lie to the *calumnies* spread about me by the *demented* Mrs Page.

À propos, Mr James Page has been *here*, and not on my account, I do assure you. He has been wooing Miss Jane Hudson, and has been sent away with a flea in his ear! It was a most curious business altogether. The supposed 'love' came from nowhere. Apparently, if he is to be believed, it sprang up from a chance meeting at the Opera to which I was a witness. It had, I must say, nothing of the marks of love, except that it led to a proposal. On her side there was no feeling at all, except indifference if not dislike, and she rejected him firmly – even, I suspect, unkindly. I have heard her give it as her opinion that he is in debt and imagined that marriage with her might retrieve his fortunes.

Can that be, Lydia? Can he by gambling or some other dissipation already have ruined the fortune he inherited from his father? If so the unattached ladies of Norfolk should be warned, especially those with independent fortunes or expectations of one. If matters are as Miss Hudson suspects, then the young man's mother and sisters are in a sad way, and likely to suffer for his profligacy. Please make enquiries, Lydia, if this is likely to prove the case, for in spite of my wrongs at the hands of Mrs Page, I retain the warmest feelings for Lizzie and her sisters.

I write hurriedly to acquaint you with my happiness, and assure you that I remain

your loving friend

Frances

The matter of Miss Weyland's engagement was in fact very much less romantic than the account she gave to her former school friend. The essence of it may be summed up in the thoughts of both of them when they separated in the grounds of Elmstead after the proposal had been made. In Mr Worsley's case they were, as he made his way back to the schoolroom, Well, that's done. Miss Weyland wandered towards the river bank feeling that, though they both knew why the proposal had come about, he could have tried to inject a little more romance and drama into it. A clergyman, Miss Weyland thought, ought to be a bit of an actor, for assuredly he was called upon to be a bit of a hypocrite.

Nevertheless, as she told Lydia Porson, the engagement was a fact, and Lady Hudson had been informed. Miss Weyland had made sure of that by telling her herself.

CHAPTER FIFTEEN

Preparing For An Explosion

4 September

A curious thing happened after dinner tonight. I am haunted by the feeling that, though things seem to be returning to normal (with the great gap inevitable after the death of Sir Richard, but of course we were used to his not being among us), what is being established is something oddly and disturbingly *wrong*, in a way I have hitherto been unable to put my finger on.

Tonight enabled me to define it a little more closely.

There is no more port after dinner when the ladies have withdrawn. I do not regret it, for it was a ceremony rather than a pleasure. It was the opportunity of a man to man conversation with Sir Richard that I valued (and sometimes feared!). Now Sir Andrew and I sit on for five minutes, for form's sake, and to enable the ladies to perform any of the mysteries of toilette that they may think necessary. Then we join them.

Tonight my pupil and I chatted desultorily on political topics, then we got up and crossed into the drawing room, where the ladies were in two groups: Jane and Lady Hudson by the fireplace, Miss Weyland and her two younger charges over by the window. Restraining my natural inclination to go over and

talk with my betrothed, I stood with Sir Andrew close to Lady
Hudson, who was pouring coffee into cups on a tray beside her.

'Coffee, Andrew?' she asked. 'Or tea?'

'Coffee please, Mother.'

Lady Hudson poured, and handed the cup to Joseph, who
conveyed it the couple of feet distance and put it beside Andrew
on the mantelpiece.

'My, Sir Andrew, I'd never noticed before you were getting
so tall. We'll be seeing you off to college in no time, won't we?
Durham, wasn't it, Sir Richard had plans for you to go to? Or
was it London?'

He smiled horribly and continued looking into his face,
apparently expecting an answer. Sir Andrew stared through
him. Joseph turned, still with the unpleasant smile playing on
his lips, and walked over to the group by the window.

'Mother, why don't you get rid of that odious man?' asked
Jane urgently.

'I can't!' said Lady Hudson fiercely . . . 'Not when your
father is hardly cold in his grave.'

I can remember no occasion when one of the servants has
made a remark of a personal nature to any of the Hudsons in
public in this way. Even Pennywear, with his long history of
service to Sir Richard and Lady Hudson, would not have
ventured beyond a remark about the weather, or some comment
on the food or the wine he was serving. There may be
households where Joseph's remark would have been a
commonplace, but Elmstead Court is emphatically not one of
them. That Sir Richard's relations in private with Joseph went
rather beyond the conventional one of master and servant is
likely, and was a matter of comment in the family and the
house, but in public the conventions were always observed.

It was as if Joseph was throwing down a gauntlet.

I may add that Sir Richard never suggested to me that the
boy should go to one of the new seats of learning, if such they
may be called. Certainly he once made an off-hand mention of
Durham, but it was no more than that. Of the college there I
know little, beyond the fact that there is some such place. The

origin of Sir Richard's wealth was in the north, and his father lived there all his days. Nevertheless the remoteness of the college hardly renders it convenient or inviting. Of London I know what everyone knows: that the college was founded as a protest against the Anglican regulations in force at the two old universities, and the dominance of the Established Church there. Without approving I can understand that some people would feel the need for a less sectarian place of education. Nevertheless I can never remember Sir Richard expressing any opinion on the subject. He was a sincere but not bigoted supporter of the Church of England. So, beyond the odd remark that Andrew was sadly unformed for Cambridge, that the men who had been to a public school would greatly outstrip him in knowledge of the world, I can recall nothing that would give any credence to Joseph's remark. I would add that Oxford and Cambridge are really the only two universities that a gentleman would consider for his son. And Sir Richard, in spite of some opinions that might be described as radical, was very much the gentleman, and one ever eager to assert his position in the world.

What was the true meaning of Lady Hudson's 'I can't'? Why does she allow Joseph this latitude? It is as if he wanted to play his part in family affairs, to influence the decisions taken. Absurd thought!

When he had finished his entry Mr Worsley meditated putting the diary back in the desk where it had used to lie. He rather thought that Joseph, having had his triumph, would have lost interest in the book. On second thoughts, remembering the gross assertiveness of the man that evening, he took the book up to the second floor and put it back into his personal trunk. As he laid it among his meagre possessions and turned the key in the lock it struck him that his final summing up of the scene in the drawing room had not been strong enough. What Joseph's words and manner seemed to him to amount to was a declaration of power over the Hudson family.

*

On the day after the incident narrated in William Worsley's diary there took the road back from Denge to Elmstead that same bundle of heavy clothing that had the look of an ambulatory Christmas pudding. This time nobody stopped to offer her a ride, but the bundle trudged on tirelessly. Though the clothing was as voluminous as before Mrs Morrissey had now no scarves over her face, and anyone passing her going in the opposite direction would have seen playing around her small mouth a very unpleasant smile – a smile of impure satisfaction.

Mrs Kate Morrissey had got the result she wanted.

She did not long delay in sharing knowledge of her good fortune. Mrs Turner, poor woman, was only informed of the outcome of whatever quest she had been on by her lodger's demeanour, which was triumphal to the point of being unbearable. All queries were fenced by Mrs Morrissey with the reply that Revelations would come 'in the fullness of time', an immeasurable time span that did not satisfy Mrs Turner at all.

However, next day Mrs Morrissey went up to Elmstead Court. It was her first view of the house, but her son had acquainted her with its main features. She had no eye for the solid mid-eighteenth-century assertiveness of its frontage, and she compared it disparagingly in her mind with the various residences of the Duke of Preston. She trudged stolidly round to the back of the house and banged on the door to the kitchen. The maid who went to the door was Bessie, the one who had announced Mr James Page's presence in the house to Jane – a pert, bright little thing. When she asked the old woman what her business was she received the reply: 'I want to see Joe Morrissey.'

'He's busy serving dinner upstairs at the moment – we're all busy with it.'

'I'll wait.'

'Was it any special business you had with him?'

'I'm 'is mother.'

She nonplussed Bessie, who against her better judgement stood aside. Mrs Morrissey stumped into the kitchen and looked around her. The place was indeed abuzz with activity, with Cook as its centre, though so firmly in control was she that she took for granted rather than directed: she had created, as all good cooks did, the perfect domestic machine which functioned so smoothly that she was able to attend to her own mysteries. Mrs Morrissey, however, regarded the operation without any visible signs of admiration, and soon, without having been asked, she took an upright chair by the fire.

'She says she's Joseph's mother,' whispered Bessie to Cook. 'Pushed her way in without being asked.'

'Then she will be Joseph's mother if she done that,' said Cook grimly. 'Always where he's not wanted, that one.' She finished whipping a bowl of cream and cast a look in the direction of the chair. 'She has a look of him too. It's not a look I like in the man, and I like it still less in the woman. Could 'ave sworn I'd seen her before somewhere.'

As the bustle began to diminish with the serving of the puddings in the dining room upstairs, others in the kitchen had time to steal glances at the bundle of bombazine over by the fire. Elmstead being no more than a village several of the kitchen staff remembered seeing her, and finally one of the upstairs maids said: 'That's 'er what's been staying with Mrs Turner.'

That jogged several memories, and by the time Joseph was free from his duties serving tea and coffee in the drawing room and had been directed to his mother when he came back to the kitchen, he found the upstairs maid in conversation with her.

'Comfortable are you, at Mrs Turner's?' she was asking the bundle.

'Very comfortable, all things considered, though it's not what I'm used to.'

'I thought Mrs Turner said as the name of her lodger was Mrs Hill,' said the maid.

'My mother was married twice,' said Joseph firmly, coming up from behind.

The maid thought that if this was so there was no accounting for men's tastes, but she was stared at so fixedly by Joseph that she was forced to withdraw. Joseph bent over the chair, planted a peck-like kiss on his mother's forehead, and the two of them began a long conversation, neither of their faces being visible to the body of the kitchen, Joseph's large body, in fact, covering all but the outer suburbs of the bundle. After more than five minutes Joseph straightened up, and his mother rose from her chair. Some of the watchers had an impression of her feeling inside her voluminous wrappings, and of something passing between the two. Then Mrs Morrissey turned towards the door.

'Joseph, where's your manners?' called Cook sharply. 'Introduce your mother.'

Joseph, unfazed, turned his bulk in the direction of the long servants' table and led his mother over to the ample lady standing beside it.

'Mother, this is Mrs Martin, our cook. Mrs Martin, this is my mother, Mrs Hill as she now is. And a very fine cook she is herself, I can tell you.'

'Oh?' said Cook, trying to be friendly. 'Are you in service yourself, then?'

'Have been in my time.'

'And where was that?'

'With the Duke of Preston. That was a top-notch establishment – all 'is residences were. Not a tuppenny-ha'penny set-up like you've got 'ere.'

Mrs Morrissey, in all her dealings, lost little time or effort in trying to make herself loved.

Joseph Morrissey prided himself on his strategic sense. Or, as he put it to himself: 'There's nobody to beat me in planning ahead.' He had regained all the confidence he had lost after his worsting at the hands of Dr McClelland. In particular his mother's visit to Elmstead Court had restored spring to his step. He went through his routine household duties with no more than half his mind on them, the other half looking ahead to a glorious future of power and prosperity.

Joseph's forward planning was in fact dictated by household routine, and amounted to little more than ringing round in his mind the third Thursday in September. That was when Pennywear was due to take his two days off a month. It was his unvarying habit to visit his brother's family in Matham, where he had a little niece he was devoted to. He always stayed overnight and arrived back at Elmstead Court in time to supervise Friday's dinner. On the Thursday, however, Joseph would reign supreme above stairs.

As the days went by his preparations for that evening were little more than an effort to be particularly pleasant to Ellen Harper, the maid who regularly helped in the serving of coffee after dinner. Since he and she had enjoyed occasional snatched sessions of sexual bliss (only occasional, for Elmstead Court was a very correctly run establishment) this was not too difficult. His pleasantness to her consisted of little more than the odd opening-up to her on a personal level, a thing which seldom happened with any of the other servants. In one such chat he confided to her: 'My old Ma's a bit of a tartar – I'm terrified of 'er meself.' This went round the staff, and went some way towards alleviating the unfavourable impression left by the lady herself.

Meanwhile Joseph continued observing life above stairs: he saw his occasional well-aimed remarks further robbing Lady Hudson of self-confidence; he observed the progress of the romance between tutor and governess, if such a tepid business could be said to make progress, or indeed to be a romance; and he saw Jane Hudson gradually loosen herself from the tutelage of Miss Weyland, and begin more and more to take herself to her late father's library and range through the books there on some scheme of discovery and self-education devised by herself.

Only in the new baronet could Joseph observe no further than the surface, where there was a new but still tentative confidence. But Joseph told himself he was not worried by Master Andrew. He'd done his business with him, and very enjoyable it had been. He could not expect any repetition now that Sir Richard had gone to his final account. But he would have his way with Master Andrew, as he would with everyone else.

On the morning of the third Thursday in September, after Pennywear had departed in the dog cart on his journey to his

brother's, Joseph rode into Elmstead. He said he had an errand
for Lady Hudson. Today, blissfully, there was nobody to account
to for his doings. He rode straight to Dr Packenham's substantial
home on the outskirts of the village. It was a beautiful red-brick
residence built in the reign of the previous queen regnant, but
Joseph had no more eye for fine architectural proportions than
his mother. He rather arrogantly demanded to see Dr Packenham
on an errand from Lady Hudson, and was immediately shown
into the doctor's study. Once there his arrogance was replaced
by an odious confidentiality.

'I'm sorry to have to tell you, sir,' he said in his footman's
voice, 'that Lady Hudson's health is beginning to give cause for
concern.'

'I – I'm sorry to hear that,' said Dr Packenham, oddly hesitant,
and playing with papers on his desk.

'To her, Dr Packenham, to her. She's doing her utmost to hide
it from the family.'

'Ah – well, after a bereavement that's perhaps to be expected.
It may be something quite small that she's exaggerating in her
mind. Out of concern for the younger members of the family,
perhaps.'

'Well, we'll hope so, won't we, sir? Everyone at Elmstead
Court is devoted to Lady Hudson. But the fact is she is very
worried. She asked if you could come and see her—'

'Oh dear. I am very busy today.'

'—as a friend. A personal visit – apparently just a personal
visit. So as not to alarm the family. She asked if you could come
after dinner, like you used to, and she could take the opportunity
to consult with you privately, whilst the family is otherwise
occupied, as you might say.'

A medical practitioner in a country district does not normally
hesitate when his presence is requested at the big house, but Dr
Packenham certainly did hesitate. And in that moment Joseph
became certain.

'Very well,' said Dr Packenham at last. 'Of course I'll come.'

Dinner that day at Elmstead Court was a nervous affair. The

long polished table in the dining room reflected the heavy and hideous epergne, the many-branched candelabrum, and the shady figure of Joseph as he moved around the table, serving and directing the maids. Perhaps it was the presence of Joseph, in place of the reassuring figure of Pennywear, that made the diners nervous. Lady Hudson made little stabs at conversational topics, and between courses her hands fluttered to her neck and she looked around her uncertainly. Anyone who remembered her ample, confident – if watchful – presence at her own table not six months before would have wondered at the change in her. She ate little, though the roast lamb was excellent. But in fact all the diners except the two younger girls seemed to lack appetite.

'Joseph met Dr Packenham in the village, and he said he intended coming after dinner,' Lady Hudson said in an unnaturally high voice during the pudding course. Joseph, at the sideboard, bent his head over a salver.

At last it was over. At a signal from Lady Hudson the ladies got up and withdrew to the drawing room. After a cheerless attempt at conversation about the approaching move to Little Burdock Sir Andrew and Mr Worsley joined them. Joseph of course was already there. He had earlier darted through the baize door for a quick visit to the kitchen, where he had found his mother.

'Hello, Ma,' he said, not bothering to keep his voice down. 'Wait 'ere till Lady 'Udson sends for you.'

'*Sends* for her?' squawked Cook, outraged. 'What do you mean? Lady Hudson would *never* interview a servant after dinner in the drawing room!'

'Oh, it's not about that that 'er ladyship wants to talk to Mother,' said Joseph airily.

When the men arrived Joseph was setting out the coffee cups. Nervous little groups had formed themselves – Mr Worsley and Miss Weyland this time over by the window, trying to find something to talk about, the younger girls at table occupied with a puzzle, all the rest around the fire. Nobody, not even the girls, had much to say to each other. Lady Hudson's nervousness was affecting them all. As Joseph was serving the last of them with coffee or tea, Dr Packenham's footsteps were heard in the hall.

'Oh – Dr Packenham – how nice – we hoped you could come.' There was no access of confidence in Lady Hudson's greeting. 'It's coffee, isn't it? Coffee, Joseph, please.'

When he had handed Dr Packenham his cup and removed the small table with the coffee things on it closer to Lady Hudson's chair, Joseph and Ellen, the housemaid who had assisted him, withdrew towards the drawing room door. There was still a flurry around the new arrival, and no one saw Joseph take a half-sovereign from his pocket and slip it to the maid.

'Bring my Ma up 'ere, then keep away,' he hissed. 'And keep everyone else away too: Lady 'Udson's orders.'

He stood, his heart beating fast, by the door, watching the three little groups in the body of the room. Minutes later he heard a flurry of skirts outside the door, and he opened it softly to admit Mrs Morrissey. He was not quiet enough, for the newcomer caught Lady Hudson's eye and she turned towards the door with both consternation and outrage in her expression.

'What—?' she began to ask.

Joseph turned, closed the door and locked it, and then swung back towards the room, where everyone was quite still and watching him.

'Now!' he said.

CHAPTER SIXTEEN

A Seizure of Power

'What in Heaven's n—' began Dr Packenham, getting up from his chair by the fire.

'Sit down!' roared Joseph. 'You're not going anywhere.' He stood firm against the door to drive home his command. 'We need you 'ere, Dr Packenham.'

The younger members of the family watched with horror as the doctor subsided into his chair.

Joseph smiled at this first victory. He left his position in front of the door and began prowling to and fro in front of it.

'One or two of you others, on the other hand, had better be gone,' he resumed, more quietly but even more menacingly. His voice had lost most of its coarse bluster, and sounded more like the voice they were accustomed to, and hated. 'We wouldn't want Miss Dorothea or Miss Amelia hearing what I've got to say, would we, Lady Hudson? Get out, young ladies!'

The younger girls, sober and frightened as they had not been since their father died, had stopped work at their puzzle and now looked towards their mother.

'Go!' she said, her voice coming out tiny and high. The girls looked at each other, then got up and scuttled to the door, which Joseph had unlocked and now held open for them. He turned, grinning evilly, to the pair in the window seat.

'And, do you know, I don't think we need you, *Mr* Worsley and *Miss* Weyland. Served your turn, you have, in amusing Sir

Richard. Had a lot of fun, he did, out of you. Set you, Mr Worsley, to writing to all the young ladies you'd known, and hardly known – Miss Bront and the rest. Watched Miss Weyland wondering which man she had a hope of catching – juggling two balls in the air and scared stiff she'd drop both. Oh, he was a great one for little games, was Sir Richard. But that little game is over and done with. If Miss Weyland wants my advice – and she could do worse, because I know when I've got the upper hand, and I know how to use it – I'd say: keep him to it. Breach of promise actions don't do any good for the prospects of them as aims to fly high in the Church, do they, Mr Tutor? And Sir Richard would be pleased: a romance cemented from beyond the grave, you might say. But that's your business. You're no more than upper servants. You're nothing. You can get out because I've got bigger fish to fry than you two!'

He backed to the door and held it open. Horrified, the two young people by the window looked to Lady Hudson. She looked down into her lap, and then nodded. First Mr Worsley, with an attempt at dignity, rose and walked in measured steps to the door. Then Miss Weyland, thoroughly frightened, scampered after him. Joseph closed the door and again stood in front of it. Suddenly everyone in the room became conscious again of the figure of Mrs Kate Morrissey. Going over to the table she took up a chair and brought it over to the door, putting it just under the handle. Then she sat down in it, black and threatening, like some prison wardress or Bedlam attendant. When she had settled herself down, spreading her drapery so the chair disappeared under her, she slowly cast her eyes around the room. Her mouth curved into a smile that was a signal of the power she and her son had over the watchers, and the contempt she held them in. Then she withdrew her face and became nothing more than a black bundle.

Jane Hudson shivered.

'Now!' said Joseph again, standing by his mother and looking bulkier than ever. 'Now for the big fish!'

He looked at Lady Hudson as if she were some great sturgeon on a silver salver and he were about to slice her up for the enjoyment of dinner guests. Then he turned to Dr Packenham, who had risen and was now standing somewhat apart, making no attempt to comfort or support the lady of the house. Joseph's mouth twisted evilly.

'When did it start, I wonder?' he asked. 'How did it start? With a glance here, a touch of the hand there? I don't know too much about the habits of the gentry. We're a sight more direct in the servants' hall, though we do it quietly for fear it might come to her ladyship's notice. Very keen on the proprieties, aren't you, Your Ladyship? So how was it, Dr P.? Did you meet up when Lady Hudson was on one of her charitable missions and when you were deigning to exercise your skills on the deserving poor? Well, you don't have to tell us. I don't know and I don't much care. What I do know is that there's been something between you for nigh on a year now. And Sir Richard knew and all!'

Something had got into Lady Hudson – something that stiffened her and gave her the courage to resist. Now that things were coming out into the open she was emboldened to raise her head and look straight at Joseph. She said nothing, but the set of her shoulders announced that she was not going to go down without a struggle, and so did the firm line of her lips. Jane, looking at her out of the corner of her eye, felt admiration. And for the first time in her life she loved her mother, felt she understood her. She too, in her way, had fought.

Joseph watched mother and daughter, then he looked down at his own mother, as if requiring a degree of admiration for his performance. The black bundle nodded approbation. Joseph smiled and turned back to his prisoners.

'He was quick, was Sir Richard, quick on the uptake. As you should have been the first to know, Your *Ladyship*. He picked up the little looks you gave each other, the whispers when you thought no one was looking. And if he didn't see, he had my eyes seeing for him. He knew, and he didn't do anything to stop it. He liked knowing, he liked having a new sort of power over you. He wanted to know how far you'd go. He calculated as 'ow you wouldn't find it that easy here in Elmstead, even in blind

Sally Birley's cottage. He thought you couldn't do much more than hold hands – was he right there, Lady H.? Or did you find a time and place now and again? Anyway, his idea was that in London things would be a lot easier. Sir Richard had his own little secret pleasures in London. He wasn't always with the politicians and the men in government offices. He thought that in London things would – how shall I put it? – come to a head!'

Jane Hudson, consumed with loathing for the sneering figure by the door, suddenly got up and went to stand by her mother, putting her hand tenderly on her shoulder.

'Why are you telling us this?' she asked in a hard, bright voice. 'You're not telling *me* anything I didn't know already.'

'Aren't I, Miss Jane? Then perhaps I will do before too long. *Sit down!*'

Jane looked at him bawling at her – ugly, leering, triumphant. She looked down at her mother, who touched the hand on her shoulder and nodded. Jane sat down beside her.

'In London I did you a service, Your Ladyship. I don't expect no thanks for it, though I may expect something else.' Joseph turned his leer towards his mother, and the bundle shook. It was laughing. 'I had information about you what I didn't pass on. When Sir Richard could spare me he set me on to watch you, but I told him I couldn't find out if you two was meeting in secret or not. I said you went to places – fine 'ouses, exhibitions, and whatnot – where I couldn't follow you, where you might leave by other entrances where I wasn't watching. I thought: this 'ere information, that might very well be more useful to me than it would be to him. Oh, I left him still very suspicious, because he knew what he'd seen, but I didn't tell him' – he paused, rubbing his hands – 'I didn't tell him about Fulton Drive, off the Edgware Road.'

If that was a blow it was one Lady Hudson took without flinching. She continued looking straight at him.

'See, I thought of the use Sir Richard could make of that information – playing with you both for a bit, then coming down hard, like he enjoyed doing, like he did with Master Andrew – and I thought that the use I could put it to was a better use than that. Better for me. I thought: Charity begins at home, like it says in the good book. So I kept mum, and I didn't tell as how I'd followed you to Fulton Drive, didn't tell who I saw letting you in at the front door, who I saw leaving the house after you'd gone. I said to meself: this 'ere's going to come in useful one day, Joseph, my lad. And it has, hasn't it just!'

His ugly, sneering face raked over them.

'I don't even know when I got the suspicion that something more was in the wind, something even I hadn't expected. But when the family got back here to Elmstead and Sir Richard's temper got worse with his health, I saw every one of you hating and fearing him more and more, and one day I thought: someone's going to do something about it. Mind you, I hadn't banked on it being young Master Andrew as brought it out into the open – though I rather think I made him regret doing that, eh, Master Andrew?'

'Sir Andrew to you. You hurt me, but you did not make me regret it.'

Andrew spoke quietly and showed no fear, but there was fear in his heart at what was coming.

'Sir Andrew it shall be, then,' Joseph continued looking at him and rubbing his hands. 'Pity you've got such a long wait before you come into the full henjoyment of your property, isn't it? Lucky for me, but not lucky for you. A shilling I got for thrashing you. I think I'll do better than that from this, don't you? Well now, I freely confess I don't know how the means of getting rid of Sir Richard came to Lady H.'s attention – oh yes: that's what we're talking about. Were the two of you walking all lovey-dovey down a country lane somewhere, and did Lady H. say: "Oh, dog mercury! Such a pretty plant!" and did the learned doctor say: "Dangerous, though. Very poisonous. Fatal to someone as has a weak heart." And did she say: "My, oh, my! Whoever'd have thought it?" How you in the gentry get your meanings across to one another isn't known to the likes of Mother and me. But what I do know, Lady H., is that you knew all about the poison, and your lover knew you knew.' He rubbed his hands again. 'I saw the look he gave you when Sir Richard died.'

'A look is nothing. It's worthless,' said Dr Packenham, in a voice that had a ring of false confidence. 'You can't produce a look in court.'

'Oh, I agree. I do agree. You need something much more solid than a look in court. Something like this.'

Slowly Joseph produced from his pocket the small bottle with black liquid in the bottom. He set it on a small table close to his hand by the door. The bottle mesmerized them all, and they stared at it in silence until they heard a small whimper from Lady Hudson. She had hoped against hope that she had imagined the fall in the level of the medicine in the bottle. Now all hope was gone. She looked down into her lap, all resistance broken. It was as if Joseph had put before them all an image of the gallows.

'Sir Richard's medicine, prescribed by you, Dr Packenham. Very nasty tasting, and ideal for hiding other nasty tastes that might be added to it. Just sitting there in his bedroom, waiting for the opportunity to arise. And on the day of his death, it does. Mr James Page arrives, wanting to talk to Sir Richard. He sends me off to see what he wants, and when he hears what it is he sends for Lady H., wanting to have a bit o' fun with her too. Lady H. likes to keep her daughter in the schoolroom, don't you, Your Ladyship? Being not too pleased at having a grown-up daughter. When they've all had their talk with Mr Page, and Sir Richard having had his fun, he dozes off, being easily tired. So Lady Hudson pretends to be worried by this – though it was perfectly normal, as she well knew: Sir Richard did sleep a lot during the day when he was in the middle of one of his attacks. Anyway, she sends me with a note to you, Dr P. – you was out at the time, otherwise I'm sure you'd 'ave come earlier – and by the time I come back the bottle's already been tampered with. So when I give him his dose at midday I'm causing the death of the man who raised me up and depended on me. Nasty, wasn't it? A horrible thing to cause a loyal servant to do.'

The conviction gripped Andrew that Joseph had known – or at the least suspected – that the medicine was to be the means to kill his father, and that he had done nothing about it precisely with a view to getting the Hudson family under his power. It could never be proved, of course, though even as he thought this there was something else at the back of Andrew's mind, something that lay there, niggling him, and refused to come forward. Some legal term . . .

'So there's her ladyship, not even in the room when the medicine with the dog's mercury in it is given to her husband. On the other hand, once it's given him she wants to be there, on her own, to get rid of the bottle that's been tampered with and substitute another from the stock we kept. She tries sending me to fetch Dr Packenham again, but I don't go. So she sends me down the corridor with a message for Miss Jane. She can't leave the room to get rid of it, because I've got one of the maids posted outside. So she hides it in a secret panel in the wardrobe she's found out about. I'll admit I never suspected you'd found out about that, Your Ladyship. Did you like what you found there, Lady H.? Did you have fun reading it? Did it bring a blush to your cheek? Or did you maybe take it in your stride? Did you think that if Sir Richard had his little amusements while he was in London, then you could have a bit o' the same?'

Lady Hudson sat on, hot of face, gazing down at her lap, her eyes full. Jane took her hand again.

'I'd be willing to bet Dr Packenham looked for that bottle when he locked himself in there after Sir Richard's death. You'd seen the inside of his mouth, hadn't you, Doctor? Seen it irritated, with ulcers starting. That's what made you sure. So you'd have looked for the bottle, I've no doubt. But you didn't find it, did you? *I found it.*'

All eyes were on the tiny bottle with its black liquid.

'I, with my hintimate knowledge of Sir Richard and his little secrets – I found it. And – do you know? – next day, after Lady H. had mounted her touching night vigil over her dead husband's body, I found it was gone. But by then I had my little sample. So I knew I could find out the truth. Oh, don't worry, Dr Packenham. Your name 'asn't been brought into it.' A shadow of recollection crossed his face, and Dr Packenham's lips tightened. How he wished he could believe that! 'Oh no, don't worry. Mother here was very cunning. You've kept away from Elmstead

Court these last few weeks, haven't you, Dr Packenham? It's been noted below stairs, you 'aving been so constant a visitor up to now. I can't say as I blame you, myself. Bit of a facer to find the woman you love has hastened her husband into the grave, eh? With a bit of advice from you to help her do it. Oh, given entirely innocently, I'm sure. But if it came to court, maybe a jury wouldn't be so sure as I am. Powerful against adultery in high places, juries are. And they expect high standards from their doctors, don't they? But, as I say, your name 'as not been brought into it . . . *for* the moment, and *for* a consideration.'

Joseph paused for a moment, and surveyed his cowering audience. In the silence a voice came from the bundle.

'They're lucky they got you, Joe, looking into it. That's my view. There's others wouldn't 'ave been so careful of the family's reputation.'

Joseph smiled, an unlovely gloat.

'Do you know, Ma, I think you're right. There's many would have gone straight to a magistrate with the hevidence I've got 'ere. Would the case have come to court? I rather think it would. Even if it hadn't, the lady's reputation would have been blasted for ever. Yes, I rather do think you've been lucky. But then, the family's been good to me – and here's me being good to *it*!'

'What do you want?'

It was Jane who spoke, her voice cutting through his odious hypocrisy and coming out harsh from her uncertainty.

'Ah – you've asked the really interesting question there, Miss Jane. I do want something. I may have given the impression to you, Your Ladyship, that I wanted to play some part in shaping this family's future. Well, that was just my little bit o' fun – something I caught from Sir Richard, maybe.' He leaned forward, an ugly expression of contempt on his face. 'I don't give a pig's fart where Master Andrew – beg his pardon, *Sir* Andrew – goes to university, or what he does with his feeble self afterwards. And I don't give a sow's fart what unlucky man lands the prize of Miss Jane's hand in marriage – her hand, along with her uppitty notions about women and their rights. He has my sympathy, but I don't give a damn who it is. No, all me and Mother's interested in is – well, in me and Mother.'

His smile around the room was a satisfied one: he enjoyed the dictating of terms.

'Blackmail,' said Andrew sharply. But suddenly, from the back of his mind where it had been lurking the phrase that had been niggling him presented itself. It was 'Accessory after the fact'. What exactly did it mean, legally? Could it be useful?

'Blackmail? Oh no, Sir Andrew. You don't frighten me with an ugly word. A proper return for services rendered, that's all me and Mother ask. Take Mother, now. I think a nice little position in the household as deputy cook would fit the bill. That's a modest demand, isn't it? It'd have to be exceptionally well paid, we'd have to insist upon that. With Mother having had a notable career as cook in the service of the Duke of Preston, a proper wage is only her due. And if Cook doesn't like it, she can get her marching orders and another be put in her place. Because at her age Mother can't be expected to do the heavy work – just give the benefit of her experience with the highest in the land.'

He looked around him again with that satisfied smile: it reminded Jane of the cat surveying the rest of the cream-bowl before getting down to consuming it.

'And what about me, I hear you ask? What do I want? Well, I'm a reasonable man – I think I've proved that today. But I do have a few little wants and requirements that I think you'd be well advised to cater for. You see, I'm not sure that I've got time on my side. Because when Sir Andrew takes over the estate I *hope* he'll be as careful of his mother's reputation as his mother is herself. I do hope so. And I think he'd be well advised to be, as well. What is it you're planning to make your career in, Sir Andrew? Hoping to be some kind of diplomat or hambassador, aren't you? And do you think it would do your career any good to be known as the son of a convicted murderess? A *hanged* murderess? Or even a suspected one? No, I rather thought not . . . Still, I've got to be careful. Plans change. And I'm sorry to say that I think Sir Andrew bears me a grudge. Most unreasonably, because I was only obeying orders. But I've got to take into account the possibility that Sir Andrew would be willing to risk his mother's reputation in order to get his own back on me. Or just to get me off his back.'

He gazed, smiling repulsively at Andrew, who sat on impassive. He's making himself accomplice to a crime, he was thinking.
Then he thought: Give him enough rope . . . But he put that
thought from him. It brought things too close to home.

'So I've got to get my just rewards before the young master
reaches twenty-one. Some time before that date Mother and I
will – shall I say evaporate? Now, as I say, I'm not an unreason-
able man: I know Lady Hudson can't touch the capital sum
because of the entail. She only controls the income of the estate
and the interest on the investments.' He twisted his mouth in self-
congratulation and looked around triumphantly. 'See, I learnt a
bit from Sir Richard, didn't I? He very graciously condescended
to talk over his affairs with me from time to time. I didn't get
so bad a grasp of things for a chap with no education, did I? So,
understanding the position, I realize that the only thing that we
can talk about is the family's income from year to year.'

He put his hand on his mother's shoulder and they both gazed
malevolently at their captives. Then Joseph bent forward his big
head and shoulders.

'I'll say *half*. I'd say that was fair, wouldn't you? Knowing
what I know. What me and Mother know. Half the income on
the estate. I suppose it'll mean a bit of tightening of the belt for
you all, but I don't think that'll do you any harm. Maybe you'll
understand better what makes poor people do what they do do.
I'll have to see the books, o' course, Lady H. To see that I get
my rights. I want to understand the whole business of the estate,
the stocks and shares, where the family's money comes from. It
can all be quite natural: below stairs they'll realize that you've
come to depend on me just as your late husband did. I was his
right-hand man, and now I'll be yours, Lady H. And I assure
you I'll never take hadvantage of my position.' He leered. 'The
favours I'm after are all financial.'

He drew himself up and walked to the centre of the room,
looking round in triumph at the little circle.

'Do we understand each other? I hope we do understand each
other. For the next few years I'm in charge. You jump to my
bidding. You're all in my control. Don't try to rebel, because

I'm a hard man when I'm crossed. Well, I think that's all I've got to say. Good night, Your Ladyship. Good night, Sir Andrew. Good night, all. It's been a pleasure doing business with you.'

CHAPTER SEVENTEEN

Postscriptum

From: *In the Service of the Queen*, Being the Memoirs of Andrew the First Lord Hudson, Sometime Her Majesty's Ambassador to the Courts of Portugal, Vienna, and the Sublime Porte, and Third Viceroy of India. Smith, Elder & Co. 1893

But, along with the death of my father, there was approaching inexorably the end of my childhood. The child who was father of the man was giving way to the man who was the product of that childhood.

Many old buffers like myself, seeing youngsters celebrating their coming of age, feel a certain condescending amusement: how much these young men have to learn, if they believe that the age of twenty-one brings real adulthood, or even real freedom from the restraints of minority!

My own feelings are very different, for they are: how late the freedom comes for these men! For me the moment came much earlier, a mere six months after the death of my father. In the entail under which I inherited Elmstead Court and the considerable wealth attached to it, my grandfather – whether in his wisdom or in his folly I leave it to the reader to decide – had stipulated that, should my father die during my minority, I should come into full and untrammelled possession of my property and fortune at the age of eighteen. My grandfather, it should be noted, had started in the woollen trade at the age of fifteen and was already a figure of some wealth and importance by the time he was eighteen. He had no patience with laws that put the constraints of childhood on those whom he considered to be already men. I had a half memory of his telling me this, dandling me on his knee, not long before his death.

That I gained control of my inheritance at that age was a matter of considerable surprise to everyone except myself. The terms of the entail had no doubt been explained to my mother at the time of my father's death, but due to her disordered state of mind she had failed to take them in. I had always been treated as younger than my years – indeed, shortly before that memorable birthday my mother had asked me: 'Is it seventeen you'll be, Andrew, or eighteen?' Perhaps also she had the shyness many good-looking women feel in admitting to grown-up children. On the day itself I confess to being scarce able to contain my excitement over breakfast. And when Mr Winterburn our solicitor rode over from Marwick to keep his appointment with me and initiate me into the mysteries of my inheritance it was only by a superhuman effort that I did not reveal my delight at my prospects to the whole household – which would certainly have been unseemly!

I should say, in justice to my mother, that she greeted my taking control of the estate with relief. She had found the exercise of an authority to which she was unaccustomed a great burden and worry. As a consequence of her inexperience there had arisen some disorder in household affairs – in particular a manservant on whom my father had greatly depended had been allowed, through my father's partiality and my mother's inexperience, to gain a greater power in the household than was right or proper. It was with great pleasure that I gave him two hours to leave Elmstead Court, notice that was reinforced by the sternest of warnings from Mr Winterburn. I watched him and his mother, for whom a place below stairs had been most unwisely found, depart from Elmstead down the avenue of elms in hangdog fashion with a heady sense of my own power and a most unChristian delight in its exercise. The man was later, I believe, among the last transports to Van Diemen's Land.

And so began the break-up of the family around which my life had hitherto been centred. My excellent tutor accepted the living of Little Burdock which was in my gift, where he performed his duties most zealously, and was later preferred to the Deanship of Winchester. Higher preferment in the Church might have come his way had it not been for a rupture with his wife which caused some scandal at the time. My mother, deeming her work done, withdrew with my younger sisters first to Brighton and later to Lyme Regis, where her charitable zeal was remarkable and effective in a way her stewardship of Elmstead Court had not been, and where she was the centre of a circle of devoted bridge and écarté players.

My sister Jane, with my encouragement, removed to London, a bold step for an unwedded lady at that time, and she educated herself to a level rare for the female sex *then*, though happily not so now. She mingled with a notable and talented circle which included Mr Dickens, Mr Wilkie Collins, and Miss Burdett Coutts. She was active in the gradual opening-up of many courses at London University to women students, and could have been principal of any of the new colleges for women at Cambridge or Oxford had she so wished, but she declined. 'Those institutions will always be *male* institutions, with a female component *added*,' she once said to me, in tones of almost loftly contempt. 'We must aim for something *new* and different.' She died two years ago, not loaded with honours, but conscious of having led a *useful* life that had changed the prospects of many of her sex.

And so, for me, to a new life – a life of power and influence in the restricted domestic sphere, but also, and more to my taste, with the prospect of playing some small part in the larger world of public affairs.

To Cambridge!